Pride Publishing books by Xenia Melzer

Demon Mates
Demon's Wish

Demon Mates

DEMON'S WISH

XENIA MELZER

Demon's Wish
ISBN # 978-1-83943-937-7
©Copyright Xenia Melzer 2021
Cover Art by Louisa Maggio ©Copyright January 2021
Interior text design by Claire Siemaszkiewicz
Pride Publishing

DEMON'S WISH

Dedication

To Wikipedia and all the people posting their knowledge there. You made it possible for me to give Sammy's nervous verbal diarrhea the credibility it needed.

Chapter One

"Is everybody set?"

Sammy looked around the group of people gathered in his bookstore. It was Wednesday, which meant there would be a book club meeting after closing hours. Their little group met at least twice every month to discuss books and interesting topics related to books, and Sammy loved it. It had formed half a year after he had opened his shop, Sammy's Book Corner, and the participants had become something like a family to him, which he desperately needed after his parents had died five years before. He gazed around to make sure everybody had their stash of cookies—this time provided by Mavis and Maribell, the two witches—along with their favorite drink.

The delicious smell of freshly baked cookies mixed with the aroma of two hazelnut toffee lattes, the sharper tang of two Chai teas—heavy on the cinnamon—and his own hot chocolate before the familiar background scent of books, both old and new, made him once again congratulate himself on buying the fancy coffeemaker and establishing the little lounging area across from his cash counter. The members of their book club were seated on the four old couches around two low tables, getting comfortable.

Sammy was especially proud of this setup, since he had found all the furniture at flea markets and had given them each a do-over. The whiskey-colored leather couch hadn't been much work. Just cleaning and treating the leather with a special balm had made the piece shine again. It now smelled faintly of beeswax, something that made Sammy crave a peppermint tea with honey every time he sat on it. The two chaises had required more effort. He had upholstered them and given them each a new cloth as well. Now customers could sit down on the colors of the rainbow to read their latest purchase. The last item was a lounger whose frame he had painted in pink then sprinkled with golden glitter for good measure. A turquoise throw made the piece stand out. One of the tables was covered in dots of various sizes and colors, and the other one had wall tattoos of Drogon and Smaug looking at each other on a black background.

Sammy was the first to admit that his artistic talent was closer to what a six-year old could produce than the fine artistry people with a real gift made, but he had done a good job with the furniture and his shop. Perhaps it was because he loved his little haven of books so much that it brought out the best in him. Except for the laptop in his office and the coffeemaker, nothing in the shop was new. Most everything had come from flea markets and garage sales, making for an interesting and charming mix of styles. Sammy had dedicated quite some time matching his books with the furniture. His antiques were stacked in open wardrobes that matched their age—or came close to it. The fantasy and science fiction books lived on shelves from IKEA, which he had sprayed silver. The romance books had found their home in old wooden wine crates that were clustered around the shop in small stacks of six to ten. Comics and manga were stashed in big boxes he had built from panoplies and painted in different hues of blue. The shop was Sammy's idea of home, a feeling that seemed to convey itself, because most of his customers were regulars and loved hanging out in the place.

Sammy looked at his fellow book club members and adopted family and felt a brief shudder when he remembered their last meeting, where Amber the banshee had insisted on providing the baked goods. She might be four hundred years old, but just like every other banshee in the world, her baking skills were those of a blind man who had to find his way in a kitchen with both arms tied behind his back. *Nonexistent.* According to Emilia, the vampire in their group, this had something to do with their magic, which allowed them to pinpoint the exact time of death for every person. Apparently, the mixture of being able to look into the future without upsetting the balance of time and still warning people of their impending end didn't go well with any kind of cooking. As to why exactly that was, Emilia couldn't—or wouldn't—tell. As the only human in a group of paranormals, Sammy had gotten used to not knowing everything. There was too much going on and he had learned soon after stepping into this world that ignorance truly was bliss in many cases where paranormals were involved. He would have preferred to know about Amber's anti-talent in the kitchen, though, before he'd accepted her offer to bring snacks.

Per group vote, Amber had been banned from ever bringing sweets to the meetings again, even though Jon, the zombie living in the cellar under the bookshop, had later confessed to Sammy that the stone-hard lumps weren't that bad, once one managed to get through the crust—the burnt, black crust that may or may not once have been sugar. Sammy swallowed hard. Just remembering the taste made his stomach revolt. And he hadn't even been able to get to the core of the—he tried to find a fitting word for the deadly pieces of ballistic bakery and finally settled for 'pastries'. Declan and Troy, the two werewolf alphas, as well as Emilia, had sharper teeth and more strength in their jaws, yet the looks on their faces when the crust gave way had been disturbing, to put it mildly.

"I don't see what's so different about these," Amber declared with a pout while holding up a perfectly shaped chocolate chip cookie. Her pixie cut with the neon green hair went well with the huge, sapphire-green earrings, the thick golden chain with various amulets dangling from her neck, the five leather bracelets with Celtic runes etched into them and the approximately twelve rings she was wearing on her fingers. Compared to her jewelry, her outfit was plain—black skinny jeans, black sneakers and a black shirt with a sparkling unicorn on it, declaring *Eat My Stardust, Suckers*.

"The difference, my dear Amber, is that these cookies can be eaten without costing you a tooth. I'm so sorry to break this to you, but your baking skills are what I imagine Terry Pratchett had in mind when he created dwarf bread."

Declan put one of the cookies in his mouth, munched on it with an expression of pure bliss on his ridiculously handsome face and gulped it down. He and Troy, who wasn't there on that day due to business, looked like everybody's wet dream. They were tall and had angular faces with chiseled jaws and sharp cheekbones, broad shoulders, slim hips, long, muscular legs and hair so thick and healthy that Sammy knew women would murder for it. Apparently, the good looks were part of the genetic makeup of shifters, but Sammy still found it almost offensive how perfect Declan and Troy were. Like two sides of a coin, one dark and dangerous, the other blond and…well, dangerous, they were a constant temptation for women and men alike. When they'd first joined the book club, Sammy had had some disturbingly hot dreams about threesomes with them and it had taken him almost four months until he had been able to put them firmly in the 'friend zone'. It had helped—once they'd felt comfortable enough to relax during the meetings—to see their true selves. Because, no matter how perfect their looks were, the two werewolves were almost annoyingly arrogant and overconfident, as was typical for alphas—or so Sammy had been told by Jon. Their saving grace was a great sense of humor and their unusual choice of favorite book—*Pride and Prejudice*. After they had confessed this, nobody in their little circle was able to take them too seriously anymore, because how could somebody who loved the perfect book be a bad person? The posturing was just that—a façade to frighten potential enemies away—and the paranormal world was full of those.

"Dwarf bread?" Amber lifted one of her meticulously plucked eyebrows, a hint of steel in her voice.

"Don't take it to heart, dear. If you want, you can come over and maybe we can teach you how to get them right."

Maribell smiled at Amber and patted her hand. The witch looked like a nice, elderly lady with her flower-print dress, the square handbag and the perfectly coiffed bun at the back of her head. Her thick black hair was infused with gray strands, and around her almond-shaped eyes — a heritage from her Asian father — laugh lines softened her features. Sammy knew better, though. Maribell reminded him of his first-grade teacher, Mrs. Smithson, who had been able to shut unruly pupils up with one stern look. Those who inspired her displeasure quickly learned that there was nothing worse than the wrath of a teacher provoked…except for the wrath of witches. And with Mavis and Maribell, the first lesson was also the last.

Amber pouted, not the least bit mollified by Maribell's offer. "I followed the recipe exactly!"

"Of course you did, dear. You're a banshee, not stupid." Mavis, who was sitting right next to Maribell, looking every bit like a loving grandmother, smiled warmly at Amber. "But baking is not about following recipes. It takes a certain passion many people lack. Being in a kitchen is a calling, not a chore."

"Then forget about the lessons. I hate being in a kitchen." Amber shrugged and, just like that, the discussion was done.

Sammy cleared his throat. As much as he loved listening to the banter between his friends, they had a serious topic ahead of them. He usually didn't like to be in the spotlight, but the things they talked about were important and deserved his full dedication. All his life he had been a nerd, happiest when he could immerse himself in worlds far removed from the harsh facts of reality, a skill that hadn't been greatly appreciated by his classmates. Keeping to himself had saved him from a lot of trouble in the past, and that was a hard habit to shake. He looked around and only saw like-minded people who understood the severity of the situation.

"Let's talk about the concept of the eternal hero as he is depicted in Michael Moorcock's *Chronicles of Corum*. Before we plunge right into the story, I think we need to discuss the concept of the hero, because I realized when I started thinking about the book how simple it seems on the surface and how complicated it is when you look closer. Who wants to start?"

Sammy looked around and saw Jon raise his hand. The zombie was notoriously shy—even more so than Sammy—and they all made a point to have him talk as much as possible during their meetings. Sammy had a suspicion that this was the only time Jon ever had any social contact. He literally lived behind his PC.

"Yes, Jon?"

The zombie started kneading his hands in his lap, a sign that he had a lot of thoughts lined up in his head and was trying to get them in order. After more than four years of regular meetings, Sammy knew how to read his friends.

"Heroes are always kind of archaic, I think—at least the ones who are successfully recognized by an audience. I mean, take *Skyrim*, the computer game. The Dragonborn is this huge, buff man with muscles and a sword and his face is obscured by a helmet with two gigantic horns. It's like the person itself doesn't matter, only what he represents."

Sammy nodded encouragingly. That was a good angle.

"I agree with Jon." Emilia's melodic voice was like a caress to the ears. Sammy would have probably enjoyed hearing it a lot more if he hadn't known that it was part of her genetic makeup as a vampire to lure in prey. She could have read the telephone book and it would have sounded like the most interesting story in the world.

"Not all heroes are obscured, but the basic archaic features are always there. For example, Aragorn, from the *Lord of the Rings*... He does look sophisticated, but when it comes to battle, he shows his feral side, which I kind of like." She hesitated. "Why do we find brute force attractive?"

"Because it gets things done." Declan waggled his eyebrows at her. Vampires and werewolves usually didn't mix, but despite Declan and Troy being alphas and Emilia being of very old vampire royalty, they got on surprisingly well. Sammy thought it was because they shared a love for books — that and the fact that they were considered odd by their own people because of the lifestyle they chose. As far as Sammy understood, it wasn't normal for two alphas to join up and start a business instead of leading a pack, finding and claiming a mate and producing babies with said mate.

Emilia sighed. "I guess it does. But then why am I affected? I can get things done, too. I'm strong enough to rip a man twice my size in half without breaking a sweat and yet, I find the idea of a hero oddly attractive."

"I think it has to do with conditioning." Declan took a sip of his espresso. "Even though society has evolved, and we're taught that brute strength does *not* solve all problems, that there are other ways to deal with things, we still like our heroes to have certain attributes. Look at all the superhero films cropping up at the moment. Not one of the actors is ugly. The hero is a concept removed from reality, a role model we know we can never fully embrace, which is probably one of the reasons why heroes like Corum die in the end."

"It does make one feel better, doesn't it? Knowing that they end just like everybody else or even worse." Mavis looked contemplative. "It's as if we need to balance the perfection we crave and attribute to them. It's a bit like having a shiny car and getting it dirty on purpose now and then, just to prove a point."

"Yes. You're right. But that still doesn't explain why even I feel my nonexistent ovaries throbbing when I see Jason Momoa on screen." Amber sounded a bit frustrated.

"Does your hole twitch as well?" Jon looked at her with a serious expression.

In any other circumstances, this question would have been considered rude, but they all were close and it was a known fact — at least for paranormals — that banshees were asexual and non-binary. They referred to themselves as females simply out of tradition. Banshees all looked more or less alike — small, about five foot four, with a fragile build that belied their strength, delicate features and long, white hair. Many of them, like Amber, tried to individualize their looks by cutting and dying their hair, wearing expressive clothes or jewelry and getting tattoos and piercings.

"Yes." She shuddered. "I usually don't have any sex drive at all, and it's not like I want Jason Momoa, the man. It's more a general longing that somehow translates into something sexual — which is kind of weird, come to think of it."

"Not as weird as you may think. In a wolf pack, the strongest wolf gets his pick and the weaker ones, especially the omegas, consider it a prize to be chosen. Their rank is directly linked to the status of their mate. Humans are the same, just like most other species. And even though banshees are a different breed, you have spent enough time around for some of it to rub off." Declan smiled, showing all his perfectly white teeth.

"I agree with Declan. Cultural interference is a stronger force than many think. And the concept of the hero is universal. It's only natural for a certain image to persevere. As far as I know, there are no stories about famous banshee heroes, are there?" Maribell stole a sip from Mavis' cup of tea. The gesture had Sammy smiling. If he ever found his special someone, he hoped he would be as happy and content with him as Maribell and Mavis so obviously were.

Amber's snort pried him from his daydreaming. "We're the ones to *tell* the hero he's on his last adventure. We don't go on stupid quests ourselves. It's hard enough being there at the right moment for the person to hear our scream."

"I can't imagine what that feels like—hearing the banshee's scream, knowing what it means and still carrying on." Jon sighed. "I guess that's why I'm not a hero."

"You're too intelligent to be one." Emilia grinned. "Being a hero requires having no imagination whatsoever. Otherwise, they wouldn't do their heroing stuff and instead hide under the covers. Because, contrary to the saying that only overcoming your fear makes you a true hero, I think it's better to not have any fears in the first place. Corum is a good example for that. Even though some of his adversaries are downright frightening, the author never dwells on him being afraid. He's too busy killing things—just like Beowulf, come to think of it."

"Yes, he's a good example, his mind set firmly on the task, no matter how much bloodshed it requires." Jon took another cookie. "And the bloodshed is always described in great detail, as if the amount of blood and gore makes the deed even more heroic."

"You have a point here. Archaic heroes have little to offer in regard to personal growth—if we discount them becoming more battle-hardened with every adventure. Take Hercules… The only thing not directly linked to his strength that he ever did was choosing between the two women who represented the two paths his life could take. He actively chose to be a hero, just like Corum actively chose to follow the call of that Celtic tribe after he had survived so many tasks. Moorcock has him do it out of boredom, which would fit nicely with Emilia's theory. Somebody without imagination has a hard time doing nothing." Declan stretched his long legs. The others nodded their consent to this analysis. When it appeared that nobody had anything to add, Sammy summed up their discussion.

"So, we agree that heroes are sexually attractive, even to an asexual species, because brute strength still has a certain appeal in our sophisticated society. They're not the sharpest knives in the drawer, otherwise they wouldn't be able to mindlessly pursue dangerous situations that normal people would never attempt. And they have to die in some way or another because a happily ever after is not what we deign to let them have. Anything else?" Sammy looked around. The discussions in the group tended to get off track more often than not and he was proud how well they had managed to stay on the topic for the evening, even though the book had just been the catalyst for a broader subject.

Declan yawned. "No. Not from me. Though we could try and find some essays about the concept of the hero and include them in another discussion."

The others nodded eagerly. Sammy loved those moments, when they decided to delve deeper into a topic, to discuss it in earnest, almost as if they were attending a class in college.

"I'm going to find some essays. Perhaps we can start our next meeting by defining the different types of heroes? How does that sound?"

"Perfect, dear. Maribell and I will see what we can find on witch heroes, though I think there aren't that many." Mavis started gathering the empty cups.

Jon got up to help her. "Could you make apple pie next time?" he asked shyly.

Maribell, who had been sitting next to him, patted his leg. "Of course, dear. As long as you promise not to forget to eat your brains."

Sammy turned around quickly to hide his chuckle. It wasn't funny, really, but listening to Maribell scolding Jon about his eating habits like a concerned grandmother would do with her grandchild felt so normal — provided he ignored the content. Jon was the first zombie Sammy had met, and apparently, they could eat like normal people, but they needed some brain tissue now and then, just like vampires needed blood. When he was sitting in front of his computer, Jon tended to forget about eating and a zombie in need of brain was not a sight for people with a weak stomach.

"I won't. I promise!" Jon sounded like an eager puppy. "I have a reminder programmed into my computer and a standing order with Larry, the butcher on Main Street. Oh, and Sammy is my backup should the alarm not work."

"Very good. Apple pie it is." Maribell looked at the cups Mavis had gathered on a tray. She furrowed her forehead in concentration and, in the blink of an eye, the cups were all clean.

"I love that trick!" Declan chuckled. "You really don't want to come over to my place and do the housework? I pay well!"

Mavis *tsked* at her fellow witch. "No, we don't. Strictly speaking, it's cheating, and we only do it here because we don't want to leave Sammy with all the dirty dishes on top of everything else. He works too much."

Sammy held his hands up. "It's fine, Mavis. I love my work, and since my apartment is right above the shop, I don't have a long way home."

"Still, I'm worried about you, dear. When was the last time you had a nice boy over for some sexual release?"

And that right there was the problem with being friends with paranormal people. They tended to be *very* outspoken about bodily needs. Sammy's ears heated up. Being questioned about his love life — or the lack of it — by a woman who could have been his grandmother was disturbing enough. Seeing the adventurous gleam in her eyes and knowing that she had probably more action between the sheets than him was just sad. The pity in the eyes of the others wasn't helping either.

"You know I'm picky. I can't just bring myself to invite some random guy over Grindr solely for the purpose of having sex, not to mention that I'd have to drive over to Helena to meet because most people don't even know where Beaconville is."

"We could always drive you. Stay close, to make sure the guy behaves." Declan shrugged.

"Wonderful. Now I feel like a prostitute with his pimps. No, I want my man to woo me properly. You know, dates before sex."

Declan snorted. "You're hopelessly romantic."

"Leave him be. It's okay for him to wait until he meets his Mr. Darcy." Emilia winked at Sammy, alluding to the best book *ever*. "And he has two healthy hands and the Internet. The relief part should be covered."

Sammy buried his beet-red face in his hands. If having friends meant suffering through comments like this, he wondered if staying a loner would have been so bad.

"Can we please talk about something else? The weather maybe? And, just for the record, I don't watch porn. I don't want to get strange ideas."

"Oh man, I'm not sure if this is sad or cute. Maribell is right. You need a boyfriend. Just work is no fun." Amber slipped into her black coat. It was April and the temperatures still dropped during the night.

"Easier said than done. I'm working on it, okay?" Sammy sank into Maribell's hug. She smelled of chocolate, a flowery perfume and, very faintly, of a strange herb he had come to associate with her. After Sammy had hugged all the females, Declan gave him a firm handshake and reassured him once more that he and Troy would be more than willing to help him out should he decide to go for Grindr, which he was determined not to do.

Jon waved at them all before he disappeared through the back door that led down to the cellar. He wasn't big on touching, because the body warmth of others always reminded him that he was no longer alive. Sammy found it sad and would have loved to help Jon, but the zombie seemed to have found some balance in his life that Sammy didn't want to upset.

When his friends were all gone, he closed the shop's front door and started cleaning up. Thanks to Maribell, he only had to put the cups back on the nineteenth-century hanging shelf and clean the coffeemaker. On his way to the stairs that would lead him to his apartment, Sammy found the trash he had meant to take out earlier in the day then forgotten. After a short internal debate, he sighed, picked it up and went to the back door.

The dumpster loomed like an alien monster in the small back alley that looked shady, even during daylight. Sammy gulped. He wasn't easily frightened, but the way the shadows seemed to move in the semibrightness of the single lightbulb over the door had him hurrying to the dumpster. After he had disposed of the sack, Sammy was headed straight back for the door and the warm safety of the house, when he suddenly heard something. It sounded like a cat going through the trash in search of leftovers and the rats that fed on the leftovers. Sammy shuddered. Some of the street cats in Beaconville were small, mean killing machines and he always tried to stay on their good side. Not interfering when one of them was on the hunt was part of the plan. He reached for the door handle, recognized a presence behind him that was most definitely not a cat, felt something soft and horrible-smelling being pressed against his nose then…nothing.

Chapter Two

"Damn it, Dre! Would you mind paying attention? We're playing a serious game here and, thanks to you, I just got blown up with a plasma grenade!"

Barion, Dre's younger brother, gave him a vicious jab with his elbow. Dre didn't retaliate, because he deserved it, for one thing, and second, he was distracted by an all-too-familiar tingling at the back of his skull.

"Sorry, little bro. Seems like someone is trying to summon me — *again!*"

Barion groaned. "Damn. The same idiots from last time?"

"Feels like it. They've been doing this all week. I'm getting tired of it."

A mischievous gleam appeared in Barion's eyes. "You gonna take care of them?"

Dre pressed the pause button on his controller, freezing the battleships on the one-hundred-ten-inch flat-screen Barion had bought only a week before. Dre was sure the thing was worth a fortune, but, as a demon prince, his brother could easily afford it. Demons were not as big on hoarding as dragons, but they weren't exactly poor either.

"I think I have to. This is getting on my nerves, and who knows what they will come up with next?"

Barion rolled his eyes. "Whoever thought it was a good idea giving humans just enough information that they are able to call us should be roasted alive."

"Good luck with that one. Father is convinced it was Great-Uncle Corriwyn, and he's fireproof...like all of us, moron!"

Barion whined. "Why would he do such a thing?"

"Because he was bored and thought it would be funny. And he had fun—still has. He answers every summoning he gets, just to mess with the humans. Damn old man should have gotten himself a mate and children at some point."

The tingling got stronger and Dre wondered what kind of spell the humans were using this time. It was a widely believed myth that demons could be summoned and controlled by a human with the right spells and magic circles. It was a belief that was very false. For one thing, only a true witch had the means to infuse a magic circle with enough power to actually *force* a demon to appear. And if she wanted to do more than just have a stare-off with a pissed demon, she had to be a member of one of the five witch clans. That narrowed the amount of people who actually did have the means to control a demon to less than two hundred. As for truly mastering a demon? He knew of three who could probably pull it off, and they had other, easier means to get what they wanted.

All ordinary humans could do was the equivalent of a phone call—or prank call, to be precise. Mostly, demons simply ignored the summoning, unless they were bored, like Uncle Corriwyn, or pissed, like Dre was. As far as he could tell, the same group of humans had been trying to reach him at least six times during the past one-and-a-half weeks. That much he could sense through the weak bond caused by the ineffective spells they were using. He got up from the bright orange leather couch that Barion thought was the latest in fashion — and who was he to argue with his hip younger brother? Dre let his knuckles crack while he contemplated how to go about this. Barion watched him with interest.

"Are you going full demon on them? I'd love to see that!"

"Shut up. I don't need comments from the peanut gallery."

Dre pulled his black silk shirt over his head. There was no need to destroy a perfectly nice item of clothing. Then he closed his eyes and allowed his true form to burst through the thin veneer that hid it. He stretched from six foot seven to over eight foot tall. The silver hair that fell down his back turned into a broad stripe of silver scales that went from his head down to his ass. Dre unfolded his wings and knocked over a vase on the windowsill across the room.

"Hey, watch it!" Barion dove forward to catch the vase before it shattered on the ground. Since one of his talents was time-bending, he'd easily managed it.

Dre held up his hands to look at the beautiful silver patterns swirling over the red skin. His fangs prodded his lower lip and the claws on his toes made a clacking sound on the hardwood floor.

"Don't you dare get any scratches in that wood, Dre! I mean it! Do you have any idea how long it took me to find the perfect planks for this room?"

Barion sounded almost hysterical, which had Dre resuming most of his human form within seconds. Nothing took the fun out of changing like the whining of an annoying little brother.

"You asked me if I'd go all demon on them."

"Yeah, but I meant outside! Not here, where you act like a bull in a china store. You know it took me ages to get the house the way I wanted it."

Dre sighed. Even though 'house' was a misleading term for the huge villa Barion had bought in the Carpathians, he knew how much work his little brother had dedicated to make the formerly run-down building splendid again. It was a little over the top for his own taste—he preferred the cozy cottage he had bought in Cornwall some three hundred years before—but Barion loved his new home and Dre would rather bite off his tongue than make his little brother sad.

"Sorry, Barion. I wasn't thinking. I'll go outside. See you tomorrow?"

Barion was still clutching the vase to his chest. "Yeah. See you tomorrow. Don't overdo it."

"Nah. I'm just going to give them a scare. I don't feel like bloodshed today."

Dre grinned at his brother before he made a cut into reality with one of the claws on his hands and stepped between space and time to follow the summoning.

* * * *

When Dre reappeared in a small, stinking room somewhere in the US, he was glad he hadn't remembered to revert completely back to his demon form, because there was no way his wings would have fit in the place without knocking the—he squinted—

remaining windows out. When he looked down at the floor where pieces of tile still stuck to the concrete that was full of disturbingly wide cracks, he wondered at which level they were and how long it would take until his weight became too much for the groaning structure beneath his feet.

"We have summoned thee, Demon Dresalantion, to do our bidding until we decide to release you again."

The high-pitched, slightly quivering voice reminded Dre why he had come to this obvious dump in the first place. He turned around to look at the five humans who had summoned him. Unfortunately, the one standing in the front chose that exact moment to throw something at him, and out of reflex, Dre reared back, which made the floor creak in a way that had him contemplating returning to Barion immediately. But, no, he was a freaking demon prince and would deal with these puny humans in a way they would never forget, buildings on the verge of collapsing be damned. He touched some of the white powder clinging to his chest, brought it to his mouth and tasted it. Salt, of course — because salt was such a good weapon against evil. He barely managed not to roll his eyes, though this one was not on Uncle Corriwyn. Somebody else had come up with that bullshit. All salt did was make meals tastier — or inedible, depending on how much of it one used. Dre looked at the humans more closely. There were five of them, and their height made him wonder if they were already grown-up. Their faces were hidden behind masks that looked like those Dre had seen in pictures showing members of the Ku Klux Klan, only the fabric wasn't white. The figure in the front was wearing black, which would have been mildly impressive if it weren't clearly terrycloth from a contour sheet. Two others were wearing a very dark blue linen that was so badly crinkled that it looked as if they had a spider's web on their faces. The last two humans kept to the back, and when Dre saw their hoods, he knew why. One had a Wonder Woman print on it, the other a colorful flower pattern that had last been in style in the seventies. Dre tried not to laugh, but it was an impossible task. His guffaw echoed through whatever abandoned building they were in, while tears streamed down his cheeks. He had to give it to Corriwyn. Humans were a source of great entertainment.

The figure in the front put their hands on their hips and glared at him, which only made the terrycloth look even more ridiculous.

"Stop it, Dresalantion! I order you! You have to obey!"

Dre stopped laughing. *The little shit wants to play games?* Dre would give him what he was asking for…and more.

"What do you want?" He tried to sound subservient but it was hard. Dre wasn't that good an actor to begin with, and despite the fun the humans had provided him, he was getting back to being pissed. The small human—Dre was positive now that it was a boy and had to be a teenager—raised both hands.

"We have brought you a sacrifice to heighten your strength for the task we have for you."

He made a step sideways and gestured to the left side of the room, where a prone form lay on the broken floor. "Have your fill then carry out our orders!"

Dre had had enough. Why did humans think a blood sacrifice was required? Demons weren't fond of human meat, since it left a strange aftertaste, and given what people chose to eat these days, that was understandable. Of course, there were some cruel demons who delighted in the fear of the sacrifices, but most of those were doing time in a cell in the demon realm. Demon society had fully arrived in the twenty-first century and his father, the king, had every intention of keeping their existence a secret. For that goal, he had implemented a number of laws that prevented demons from screwing up in the human world while their society profited from the human inventions at the same time.

He eyed the boy while he made a deliberate step outside the chalk circle the teenagers had drawn on the floor. It looked more like an egg than a circle anyway. *If they have to mess with me, why can't they at least do a decent job at drawing? It isn't that difficult, is it?* Even the old Egyptians had managed to get a circle straight, no pun intended. All someone needed was a piece of rope and a stick. *Simple, really.* The boy was now jumping up and down, throwing more salt at Dre.

"I command you to step back into the circle! I *command* you!"

Very slowly, Dre pulled back his lips and let his fangs grow out. A whimper resounded from behind the boy and Wonder Woman and Floral Pattern ran for the door. He let his hair turn into scales, which took care of the linen cloaks. When he turned his eyes a shade of crimson, the terrycloth-draped boy shrieked, spun around and followed his friends through the empty doorframe with the rusty hinges sticking out. Satisfied with the hasty retreat of his summoners, Dre turned to the person on the floor. Two steps and he was kneeling next to the body. Very carefully, he grabbed the shoulder and rolled the person onto their back. Two huge, beautiful eyes looked up at him—one blue, the other a deep brown. Thick black curls framed an angular face that was definitely masculine and yet strangely ethereal, like he was an angel—which was bullshit, since angels weren't all that ethereal. Horny little fuckers, most of them. The full lips quivered, and a tear slid down the lightly chocolate-colored skin.

"Please, don't kill me."

Dre swallowed hard. He usually wasn't attracted to humans—too fragile for his taste—but this one? This one made his heart thud a little harder than usual.

"Don't be afraid. I would never kill an innocent."

The look in the still-teary eyes told him the man didn't believe him. Dre concentrated and his fangs receded, the scales turned back into hair and the red in his eyes bled out. He knew he would never really look human—more like a meta-human or as if he were taking too many steroids—but at least he had a familiar shape now.

"I promise that you're safe. What's your name?"

The huge eyes widened even more. "I'm not sure I should tell you. Names have power."

Dre frowned and tried to get his thoughts in order. The boy was clearly frightened, but not as terrified as he should have been when confronted with him changing his shape. He had expected the boy to pass out, yet here he was, staring at him with suspicion under the fear and a clear knowledge about certain precautions, like never telling a stranger your name.

"You're right. Names do have power. You know about"—Dre hesitated for a moment then settled for—"the paranormal world?"

The boy sighed. "Yes. Sometimes more than I'd like." He leaned his head back on the dirty floor and closed his eyes for a moment. When he opened them again, a strange determination had almost completely overridden the fear. "May I ask what you are?"

Dre lifted a brow and gestured back to the badly drawn chalk circle. "Make a guess." He grinned in an attempt to soothe the young man further.

"What do you mean?" The human tried to get into a sitting position and Dre hurried to help him. His hands were tied in front of him with a length of clothesline.

"Shall I help you with this?" Dre pointed at the man's bound hands.

For a moment he seemed to be confused, but then he held his arms up. Dre let one of his claws slide out to cut through the clothesline. The pieces fell into the young man's lap and he started massaging his wrists while he looked around.

"Thank you. Now what am I supposed to guess?"

Dre rolled his eyes. Perhaps the teenagers who had summoned him had hit the guy over the head, because he didn't seem to be the brightest light in the chandelier.

"You wanted to know what I am. Look around you. Chalk circle—"

"That's not a circle. That's an egg." The young man squinted at the floor, where the chalk markings were. "And it's pink!"

Dre took a closer look and, really, the chalk was pink. How he hadn't realized that before was beyond him. Though he had been pissed, and he tended to get tunnel vision when that happened.

"Okay, you're right. It's a pink chalk egg with scary symbols."

"Not that scary. Some of them are wrong. I mean, look at that one over there. It should have two loops instead of three. And the four lines at the center? If whoever drew this tried to summon a demon, they should have spent a bit more time studying their basic mathematics, because you need parallel lines, not crooked ones. And..." The young man trailed off. Very slowly he turned his head to Dre, his gaze traveling from his navel up to his face. "Holy shit. You're a demon!"

Dre bowed with a flourish. He could hear the fear creeping back into the young man's voice and he wanted it gone again. He had liked the scholarly tone that the guy had used when he'd examined the circle way better.

"At your service. And as I said, don't be afraid. I swear, no harm will come to you."

Different emotions flickered across the face of the young man. There was the fear again, but also caution, which Dre thought was good. A human could never be careful enough when dealing with paranormals. Mixed in with those emotions was a healthy dose of curiosity fighting to be heard. After a few moments, curiosity apparently won out. The young man held out his hand.

"My name is Sammy — and I'm human."

"Nice to meet you, Sammy. I'm Dre, which is short for Dresalantion. And I'm a demon."

Dre took Sammy's hand in his own and marveled at the softness of the skin and how completely his huge paw swallowed Sammy's much-smaller hand. Sammy seemed to notice it, too, and for a moment, they both just stared at their connection. Dre was the one to break the silence first.

"How did you get here?"

Sammy scrunched his pert nose. "To be honest, I don't know. One moment, I was taking out the trash after our book club meeting, and the next, something stinking was pressed against my nose. I woke from the sound of your footsteps on the floor."

Dre sighed. "So, you probably don't know who took you?"

Sammy shook his head. "No. I did hear them shrieking just now, but I was still too dazed to realize what was going on."

"Pity. They should pay for what they did."

Dre was still convinced Sammy's abductors were underage, and he would have loved nothing more than to teach them a lesson.

"They're dabbling with occultism. If you haven't frightened them off, they will soon get another lesson."

Sammy sounded a bit sad.

"Don't tell me you feel sorry for them?"

"Not really. I mean, they kidnapped me, and I'm not naïve enough to think it was for friendly reasons, but they clearly have no clue what they're doing, which means they won't survive for long. And we won't either if we don't get out of here. I don't like the sounds this building is making."

Dre didn't know what to make of Sammy. He didn't seem too frightened anymore, and the way he talked about his kidnappers showed that he knew quite a lot about the paranormal world. He sounded pragmatic, and yet Dre could sense an innocence in Sammy that he usually associated with children. And as if this contradiction weren't odd enough already, there was also Sammy's slender build that spoke to something inside Dre, as well as a deep sadness in his eyes that hinted at yet another secret of the young man's.

Sammy slowly got up and had to grab Dre's arm when he suddenly started swaying. Dre steadied him by slinging his arm around Sammy's waist. This brought their bodies even closer and, despite the filth all around them and the traces of fear and adrenaline still lurking in Sammy's system, Dre got a whiff of his natural scent and felt a shiver down his back. Unlike shifters, demons didn't recognize their true mates through scent, and Dre had always wondered how some pheromones in the air could make a shifter go crazy. But when he inhaled the spicy aroma of pine needles and cinnamon wafting from Sammy, he could imagine what it had to be like. The young man's scent was *pleasant*. Dre realized he had been staring at Sammy with his mouth open and tried to downplay his reaction.

"Easy there. Whatever they used to knock you out must be still in your system. Do you want to sit down on"—Dre gazed around—"that comfortable-looking pile of debris over there?"

Sammy chuckled. "Looks tempting. To be honest, though, I think we *really* should leave here. I'm not too sure how much weight the floor can still handle, and you're awfully big. No offense."

"None taken. Let's get you out of here."

Without waiting for Sammy's response, Dre lifted him in his arms. He figured that was the fastest way to leave the building without using his usual means of transportation. Somehow Dre got the feeling Sammy wouldn't appreciate a trip through time and space at this moment. Sammy yelped in surprise and slung his arms around Dre's neck, which felt better than he cared to admit. It was also strangely comforting that Sammy seemed to feel safe enough to cling to him.

"Wow, your skin is almost burning."

"Perks of being a demon. We're never cold."

"Like a heating blanket. Must be nice during cold nights."

Dre raised a brow while he tried to move gracefully through all the debris scattered around the abandoned building. Now that he was out of that tiny room, he realized he was on the second floor, according to the faded sign on one of the walls. In his search for a staircase, he turned right, where the floor seemed to be a little less cluttered.

"Did you just compare me to an electric device?"

Dre could feel Sammy's grin against the skin on his neck and couldn't suppress his own. Sammy was obviously relaxing more and more in his company, and he liked it.

"You have to admit it's kind of an obvious comparison. And heating blankets are a great invention, first used in the 1900s, but back then they were still kind of clunky and considered an oddity."

Dre was so baffled by this completely superfluous piece of information that his mouth hung open. "An oddity?" was all he could say.

"Yes. They started getting more attention in 1921, when they were used to keep tuberculosis patients warm. From then on, the heating blanket started its triumphal march to popularity, and in 1936, the first automatic electric blanket was invented. That basic design didn't change until 1984, when the first thermostat-free blanket was introduced to the market."

"So I'm a thermostat-free blanket?" Against all odds, Dre was having fun with this. He was a sucker for useless knowledge himself, but he hadn't known about the heating blanket.

"I'm not sure. Do demons have thermostats? It would make sense, since you're so hot—no pun intended."

Sammy obviously tried his hardest to sound serious, but there was a hint of laughter in his tone that Dre found almost irresistible. Sammy sure was an interesting human.

"You're aware that I'm an almost-eight-hundred-year-old demon who just saved your skinny ass from being sacrificed and you want to know if I have a thermostat on my body?"

He must have sounded harsher than he'd intended, because Sammy shuddered, and Dre instantly regretted his words, even though he had meant them as a joke. "I'm sorry. I shouldn't have said that. You must be in shock, and I blabber like an insensitive asshole."

"It's fine. I *am* in shock, but I'm also known for having a terrible brain-to-mouth filter and being horribly inappropriate. And, if you haven't noticed yet, I tend to divulge my wisdom when nervous. My social skills are abysmal. You did save me, so thank you…again. And I'm sorry for comparing you to a heating blanket."

Dre pressed Sammy's body a little closer to his chest when he finally found the stairs and started a slow, very careful descent toward the ground floor.

"I don't mind. I wouldn't mind being your heating blanket, if you wanted it." It was a mild attempt at flirting, meant to distract, but Sammy seemed to take it quite seriously. He leaned back a bit to look directly into Dre's eyes, his expression so serious that it fooled Dre until Sammy opened his mouth.

"You know, relationships based on intense experiences never last."

The derelict staircase groaned when Dre came to an abrupt halt.

"Tell me you're not quoting Annie from *Speed* here!"

"I'm not quoting Annie from *Speed* here," Sammy deadpanned. Then he broke into a broad smile. "I'd have never guessed that a demon would know the film."

"Are you kidding?" Dre started walking again, very mindful of where he was treading. "That film's a classic. I've seen it at least fifty times."

"So there are cinemas in hell?"

"Not to disappoint you, but I don't live in hell — well, at least not the kind the Christians invented. It's quite cozy, actually." Dre hesitated, not sure how to breach the topic he wanted to talk about. "But I assume you probably knew that already. Drugs aside, you seem awfully relaxed for somebody who just narrowly escaped becoming a sacrifice and is now in the presence of a frightening, clearly non-human creature."

"If I told you this was a side effect of the drugs, you wouldn't believe me, would you?" There was a hint of laughter in Sammy's voice. Okay, the boy obviously was over his initial fear. Mission accomplished.

"No. I'm a demon, not stupid. Out with it. What's your secret?"

They reached the ground level, and after a quick look at the floor, Dre decided it was safe to let Sammy stand on his own feet. He did keep an arm around his waist, though, in case he got dizzy again. Sammy was apparently grateful for the support, because he placed his hand on Dre's biceps when they started walking toward the exit of what must have been some kind of apartment block. And if Dre weren't completely mistaken, which he rarely was, then Sammy had discreetly sniffed him while he'd put him down.

"To be honest, I don't know what my secret is. I guess I kind of attract paranormal beings. As you may have guessed already, I've always been a nerd, the kind who reads all kinds of books and knows stuff nobody else is interested in, so, therefore, has no friends or social life to speak of. After my parents died, I opened a bookstore, and before I knew it, I was the go-to specialist for antique occult books and Japanese manga. Don't ask me how those go together because I myself don't know. It just happened. I started a book club with two adorable older ladies who turned out to be witches. Within a year, a zombie, two werewolves, a banshee and a vampire joined. The zombie now lives in my cellar behind his computer and only comes out for the meetings. Two weeks ago, the banshee tried to kill us all with ballistic pastries. I still haven't found out what she had planned to bake originally, because those lumps of blackened sugar could have been anything. The vampire comes from an old European coven and is training to become a carpenter, of all things. The werewolves are alphas without a pack who make more money in a week than most people see their entire lives and they have a secret crush on Jane Austen." Sammy took a deep breath. "As you can see, I'm used to oddness. I knew demons existed, but I always thought you liked to stick to your own kind...like old vampires."

Dre couldn't believe it. He stared at Sammy open-mouthed. "You deal with Japanese manga? There are a few I want to get my hands on."

Sammy's face lit up. If there had been any fear still lingering, it was apparently completely gone now, evaporated in the joy of sharing a hobby.

"You like them too? Great. Why don't you come over to my shop sometime and we'll see what I can do for you?"

Dre grinned happily. "Deal. And since we're talking about favors already…"

"Are we?" Sammy lifted a brow.

"Man, if you can get me the manga I'm after, we're definitely talking favors. Big ones. Anyway, since I'm here and in a good mood, I'll grant you a wish. How does that sound?"

"A wish?"

"Yes, you know… As in, tell me what you want, and I do it for you…the reason why humans summon demons."

Sammy appeared to be confused by Dre's generous—and completely atypical—offer, even though the boy probably didn't know how unheard of it was for a demon to offer something freely. "First of all, I thought it was djinns who grant wishes, not demons. And second, from what I saw, the spell wasn't done correctly. Why would you freely offer me something that is usually taken from you by force?" There was a tenderness in Sammy's voice that touched something deep inside Dre, yet another layer to the mystery Sammy posed. He cleared his throat to mask how moved he was.

"Well, you're right about the djinns. Wishes as such are their business, but you can't summon a djinn. You have to find their lamp, which is quite difficult. The things people want from demons are usually a bit more—let's call it 'hands-on'—but the principle is the same, basically. Not that I'm anything like a djinn... They're nasty. Devious. Cunning. I'm nice...or try to be. And as to why I would be willing to grant your wish, it's because you're a victim in this, because you quoted *Speed*, which happens to be one of my favorite movies, because you made me laugh and because you didn't let your initial fear cloud your judgment about me. You gave me a chance and trusted me. That doesn't happen often...like never."

Sammy sighed deeply. The smile he gave Dre was bittersweet. "That's very nice of you, Dre. Unfortunately, the only thing I really wish for cannot be granted by even the most powerful demon. As for everything else, I'm happy. There's nothing I need or want so badly that I would ask you to give it to me." Sammy took Dre's hand and squeezed it. "But if you would visit me at the bookstore, I'd be thrilled. If you want, you can come to the next book club meeting. It's next week and we're discussing the concept of the hero. I have a feeling you'll fit right in."

Dre stared at Sammy...then he stared some more. *A human without a wish.* That was an absolute novelty. It piqued his interest in Sammy in a way he had never felt before.

"Thank you for the invitation. I'd love to come. Do I need to read a certain book?"

"We took *The Chronicles of Corum* as our base, so to speak, but the discussion has already moved to more general grounds."

"I'm going to read it. I want to be prepared." Dre looked around. "Do you have any idea where we are?"

Sammy nodded. "It's the old industrial block of Beaconville. It was built in the sixties, when they found oil here, but the field was so small that it dried up within ten years. The factories were closed and, for some reason, the people who lived here left as well. Most of them moved to the southern part of Beaconville. Anyway, we have to go in that direction" — he pointed — "to get to the road. Perhaps we can stop a car, but I doubt it. It's too late for that. I'm afraid we have to walk the entire way."

Dre split his lips into a smile. Since Sammy had relaxed so obviously, he could risk showing off a bit. "You're with a demon. We don't walk." He pulled Sammy against his body. "Imagine your kitchen."

The picture of a small, yet tidy kitchen with white tiles on the wall, a scrubbed wooden floor and a trim of ornate flowers flashed through Dre's mind. Demons weren't really able to read minds, but when a human concentrated on something, they could pick up on it. Dre used the picture as his map and simply stepped into its counterpart in reality. Sammy gasped softly in his arms and looked around as if he had never seen his own kitchen before.

"*Wow*. How did you do that? I could get used to traveling this way."

Dre chuckled. "That's a secret." When he saw the disappointment in Sammy's face, he hastened to add, "But I can take you on a trip next time we meet, okay?"

"Okay." Sammy smiled a bit nervously. "I'd ask you to stay and have a coffee with me, but I'm afraid I'm too tired." He looked down on the floor, an adorable blush on his cheeks. "But I'd love to see you again — if you don't mind."

"I don't mind at all. I mean, how can I say no to somebody who likes *Speed* and manga? We have an obligation to find out what else we have in common."

Dre was surprised to find that he meant what he said. He *wanted* to find out more about Sammy.

"So…see you tomorrow?"

"Yes. See you tomorrow."

He winked at Sammy, cut time and space open and vanished.

Chapter Three

"Sammy? Sammy, are you okay, dear? You look horrible!"

Mavis' soft voice pried Sammy from the trance he had fallen in in front of the coffeemaker. He was so tired that it took all his willpower to force his eyes open. After Dre had left him the night before, Sammy hadn't been able to get any sleep at all — not because he wasn't exhausted, but because every time he closed his eyes, he saw Dre's handsome face and delicious body, which was unnerving, to put it mildly.

Sammy knew he wasn't perfect boyfriend material. He was too shy, neither flashy nor twinky, and his two-colored eyes were often considered weird. Add to that his tendency to either say nothing at all or bury his conversational partners under an avalanche of knowledge nobody needed to know — as the heating-blanket blabbering had evidenced — and he was probably the very definition of an anti-date, if a thing like that existed. Getting a crush on a demon who was so far out of his league that he'd need the Hubble telescope to see him was counterproductive to finding 'some nice boy', as Maribell had stated the day before. The only problem was that there were probably no 'nice boys' out there who would even think about going out with him, not if they weren't drugged.

Sammy could practically watch his self-esteem going down the drain. It was never that stable to begin with, but after the events of the past night, it had taken a nosedive. Maribell and the others were right, though. He needed to get a life outside the bookstore. Sammy was also pretty sure that having the hots for a demon wasn't what Maribell had had in mind either. There was also no avoiding telling Mavis what had happened, because the woman was like a bloodhound when it came to the embarrassing private parts of his life.

"I'm fine, Mavis. Just tired. I had an interesting night."

"Discussing the concept of the hero? Please!" Mavis snorted in a very un-ladylike way.

"No, afterward. I got abducted and—"

"Sammy, if this is a prank, you'd better stop it now. If not, I need something the person who did it has touched."

Sammy actually felt a chill going down his spine at the change of tone in Mavis' voice. She might look like a nice old grandma with her gray hair, the old-fashioned clothes—she was actually wearing a plaited apron over her light blue floral dress today—and the ever-present basket with her knitting, but underneath that reassuring exterior hid a powerful witch who could kill with a look...literally.

"No, there's no need for that. As I said, I was abducted, but I don't know who did it. And I don't want you to go ballistic on an innocent."

"Don't you worry about innocents, dear. I would always verify first." The smile on Mavis' lips was a little odd, as if a shark and a granny were doing it at the same time and somebody had overlaid the two pictures. Sammy was glad to be on her good side.

"Anyway, when I woke, I was in some derelict room somewhere in the old industrial block, my hands tied, and there was this huge demon who scared my kidnappers away, freed me then carried me out of the building."

"Sammy! How do you always end up in situations like this? A demon? Really?"

"Hey! It wasn't me who summoned him!"

"And you will never try... Understand? Demons are a complicated lot and it's sheer luck you're still alive. What happened?"

"He didn't want to devour my soul, if that's what you're asking. He's pretty nice, actually. And he knows *Speed*."

Mavis rolled her eyes. She looked very serious when she finally spoke. "Sammy, he may have been nice yesterday, but you should never trust a demon. They see the world very differently from us, and you can never tell what will make them laugh and like you or throw them into a rage and eviscerate you. A demon on a rampage is *not* a pretty sight."

"So, uhm, you're saying it was a bad idea to invite him over for our next book club meeting?"

"You did *what*?" Mavis' voice increased in volume. Sammy gazed around quickly, but the shop was empty. "Sammy, are you aware that not even Maribell's and my powers combined are a match against a demon? None of us can protect you, or ourselves, for that matter, if he decides he rather wants to bath in your blood than discuss a book."

Sammy shook his head. "No, Mavis. Dre is nice. He would never—"

"Dre? Is that his name? Never heard of a demon called Dre." Mavis furrowed her forehead. "Perhaps you have only imagined everything? That would be great. Well, I suppose not so much in terms of your mental health, but I'd rather find you a good shrink than have you playing with a demon."

Sammy looked down at his hands. He felt like a three-year-old who'd just got scolded by his granny for trying to pick out hot chestnuts from the oven without gloves. "Uhm... I guess now is a bad time to tell you that Dre is just short for Dresalantion?"

The look on Mavis' face would have been priceless if Sammy hadn't picked up on her obvious worry by then, which in turn made him re-evaluate everything that had happened the night before. Dre had seemed so nice. And nobody that good-looking could be evil, right?

"Did you just say Dresalantion?"

Sammy nodded miserably. "Yes. Who is he?"

"Just the second son of the demon king." Mavis waved her hand dismissively, but Sammy could see a hint of fear in her lively blue eyes. "You need to tell me *exactly* what happened between the two of you. Don't leave anything out!"

Sammy gulped. All of a sudden, inviting Dre to the bookstore didn't seem like such a good idea anymore. Why did these things always happen to him? It was almost as if he had a big neon sign over his head, saying *You're a dangerous, paranormal creature looking for some fun? Come here!* It had all started after he'd bought the bookshop and sometimes it made Sammy wonder if something was wrong with the building, though it did seem pretty normal all the time. There definitely weren't any ghosts living there—just Jon in the cellar, but he paid rent, so Sammy was sure that didn't count. On the other hand, zombies were dead as well, so perhaps it *did* count and nobody had bothered telling Sammy. He had to ask Jon if he sometimes felt the urge to walk around the house rattling some chains.

"Sammy, focus, please!"

Mavis' voice reminded Sammy that he hadn't answered her question yet. He took a deep breath and tried to gather his thoughts.

"As I said, I woke when Dre scared my kidnappers off. Naturally, I was afraid at first, but when he approached me, he said he would never harm an innocent. Then he cut the rope around my wrists and carried me downstairs. We talked about *Speed* and Japanese manga, and he offered to grant me a wish, saying he was already here anyway."

"He offered to grant you a wish? No strings attached?" Mavis looked stunned.

"Dre said it was because I made him laugh and didn't judge him, despite my fear."

"What did you wish for?" There was something in Mavis' eyes that told him she already knew the answer and felt sorry for him. She patted his forearm with her warm hand. Sammy felt tears welling up and a sob blocking his throat. With all his willpower, he fought down the grief over the loss of his parents. Five years and he still missed them as if it had only happened yesterday.

"I didn't wish for anything. I know the dead can't be brought back, and there's nothing else I need badly enough to use magic to get it. I know those things always come with a price."

"Which is *always* more than you can afford, especially when it comes to wishes—and even more so when it's a demon granting it." Mavis sighed. "There's nothing much we can do at the moment, except hope and pray to any deity who might listen that he's already lost interest in you."

Sammy didn't know why, but the thought of Dre losing interest in him made his stomach twist.

"Is he really that dangerous?"

Mavis tapped her right index finger against her lower lip, a sign that she was considering her answer very carefully.

"I haven't heard anything bad about Dresalantion yet. He seems to be okay for a demon. The problem is that, unlike werewolves, vampires or any of the other paranormal beings who live among humans, demons have absolutely no human traits, and they aren't close enough to humans to understand their motives and vice versa. Whenever a human gets killed by a demon, it's mostly not because demons are naturally aggressive. They are, but they are good at holding back. No, usually there's some kind of misunderstanding involved that would never occur, say, with a shifter. Demons are more or less immortal and often bored out of their mind. In their eyes, humans are a source of entertainment. If Dresalantion has offered to grant you a wish without any strings attached, then I think his interest in you might be real. Still, we need to be very careful. Do you understand?"

Sammy nodded, a bit dazed. He couldn't remember when Mavis had last spoken so seriously to him, if ever.

"I'll keep that in mind."

She patted his arm. "It's fine, Sammy. What's done is done. Let's see how well your demon can adapt to our little group. And, dear, you should get some sleep. The way you look at the moment, not even those sex-crazed hunks on Grindr would want to have a piece of you, which is a shame."

She winked, picked up her basket and was out of the door before Sammy could react to that painfully accurate non-compliment. He wondered if, and when, Dre would come today and if he had the time to put some cucumber slices on his eyes. They were supposed to make eyes look all young and vital. *Or is that teabags? And which tea? Wet or dry?* Surely not dry? Though it hardly mattered, because Sammy knew the moment he closed his eyes, he would instantly fall asleep. He had to find something to keep him awake. Thinking about Mavis' words sure helped, since he felt torn. His rational mind told him to listen to Mavis and trust her. She was an experienced witch, who no doubt knew better than him about the dangers of the paranormal world. His gut argued that Dre had been nothing but nice and deserved the same chance Sammy had given the other members of his paranormal social circle. His libido wanted to know why he even contemplated backing away from the finest male he had met in…ever.

Sammy was not an aggressive suitor, never had been. Thanks to his loving parents, he had come to terms with his sexuality almost immediately after he'd realized that he wasn't like most of the other boys, who liked girls. He had crushed on guys during high-school and college but had never gone farther than a hand job. Somehow it hadn't felt right, and his father had reassured him to do these things in his own time. Now Sammy was a twenty-five-year-old virgin with more emotional baggage than people his age should have, attracted to a hundreds-year-old demon who probably saw him as nothing more than an amusing distraction along the way.

Sammy groaned inwardly. When it came to dampening his mood, nobody did a better job than he did.

The wind chimes he had hung up instead of the usual bell let out its musical tones, alerting Sammy to a customer. When he looked up, his breath caught in his throat. In broad daylight Dre looked even better than he had the night before. He wore faded blue jeans, heavy biker boots that looked well-worn and a sinfully tight, black long-sleeve that hugged his upper body like a second skin. Sammy itched to touch the demon and see for himself if the shamelessly displayed muscles were as hard as they seemed. Dre's lips curved upward in a bright smile, and for a moment, Sammy saw a flash of fang, reminding him that he was dealing with a non-human, potentially dangerous person, not just an unbelievably good-looking hunk. The sharp teeth would have probably intimidated him more if he hadn't gotten used to seeing them on a regular basis from Declan, Troy and Emilia. As terrifying as it had been the first few times, now it was part of his reality. Sammy smiled back.

"Hello, Dre. I wasn't sure if you'd come."

For a moment Dre appeared to be confused. "I said I would. And hello, Sammy. It's nice to see you again, though I have to say you look a bit tired. Yesterday must have been stressful for you."

"No, it's fine. I just couldn't sleep because I was so excited. And now I'm contemplating if it's a good idea to have another cup of coffee."

Dre seemed to mull this over. "How many have you had already?"

Sammy sighed. "Don't ask. I stopped counting when I reached my fourth latte. That much coffee can't be good."

"You're right. I'm not much of a coffee drinker myself, but I know humans have a different reaction."

The word 'human' reminded Sammy of what Mavis had told him about demons. He felt torn, and it must have shown on his face, because Dre looked at him sharply.

"Sammy? Did I say something wrong? I'm sorry if I offended you. It's just—"

The obvious concern in Dre's voice made Sammy feel guilty and he raised his hand to stop the demon from saying more.

"No, that's not it. I'm used to the way paranormals refer to humans. It's just… You know, one of my witch friends was here before you came and, well, she said demons are dangerous. She got very nervous when I told her you'd come today, and believe me… There's not much that can make her nervous. But I like you, a lot, and now my brain's having a discussion with my heart and… I'm really fucking this up, aren't I?"

Sammy shot Dre a reproachful look. The demon was clearly trying hard not to laugh and failing miserably. He made several attempts to speak and finally managed after a serious coughing fit.

"No, you aren't. It's just— You're so damn honest. And even though you're worried, you're not frightened, which means a lot to me, but that also means your witch friend is right being worried about you, because when the instinct of self-preservation was handed out, you were clearly occupied with something else."

Sammy stared at Dre wide-eyed. "So, you *are* dangerous?"

Dre's answering smile was definitely predatory and sent a lustful shudder down Sammy's spine.

"What does your gut tell you?"

"That you would look damn good in my bed." The words were out before Sammy could think about or stop them. He cringed and felt heat infusing first his cheeks then his entire body. "Did I just say that out loud?" Sammy hid behind his palms.

"Oh yes, you did." Dre's voice sounded raspier, deeper than it had just moments before. Sammy risked a quick glance through his fingers and found the demon's eyes had turned a deep crimson, which did some pleasant things to his nether regions. Sammy groaned. This day was getting worse by the minute. Through the narrow gap between his index and third finger, he saw Dre licking his lips with a tongue long enough to have Sammy's entire body tingling.

"And I love it, because I'm thinking the exact same thing."

Sammy shuddered. "This is only the second time we've met! We should be awkwardly trying to find out if our feelings are mutual, not discussing...matters of the bed. And Mavis said you're dangerous!"

Dre grinned. "Oh, I *am* dangerous, Sammy. I'm known to play mean *Halo* matches, and men romanced by me are spoiled for everybody else."

"You play *Halo*? Great, we should have a match, because I'm quite notorious myself. Wait! What do you mean, *men*? As in plural?"

At least Dre had the decency to look a bit flustered. "Uh, what I wanted to say was... You see, I'm a bit older than you...and, well, I'm considered a grown-up by my people..."

Now it was Sammy who had to fight against laughing out loud, and just like Dre, he lost the battle. Between hysterical giggles, he managed to say something. "I...know you're older. I don't expect you to be...uh, untouched. It's just...the idea of you being with somebody else. I don't like it." The last words came out with more emphasis than Sammy had intended, and his face heated up even more. He groaned.

Dre touched his forearm lightly with his big hand, seemingly not sure if the gesture was welcome. Sammy wasn't sure either, but his body operated on automatic and he buried his face in the crook of Dre's elbow. A heavenly scent like ripe strawberries in the sun with a hint of dark chocolate wafted into his nose and Sammy calmed. He was almost sure he'd caught the same scent from Dre night before, but then again, his own body had had a rather ripe aroma and the abandoned building had reeked of all kinds of decay and rubbish. Dre landed his other hand on Sammy's back, rubbing soothing circles between his shoulder blades.

"If it's any consolation, I think we can now say our feelings are mutual, and I don't think it could have been any more awkward. So how about we consider this part of the dating script dealt with and you tell me your favorite city."

Sammy looked up, still unsure what he should think but too enraptured by Dre's scent and the pleasant warmth that was spreading through his body from the places where the demon touched him to try and pull away.

"My favorite city?"

"Yes, honey. For our first date, I want to take you somewhere special."

"We're having a date?" Sammy had problems keeping up with Dre.

"We are. Unless you don't want to go on a date?" The hint of insecurity in Dre's voice melted Sammy's heart.

"Oh, I *so* want to go! I just can't believe this is really happening. I mean, you're beyond gorgeous and I'm just...me."

"Which is all I want." Dre traveled his fingers down his spine, and for a moment, Sammy thought he would melt under the touch.

"Rome. I like Rome."

Dre smiled encouragingly. "Have you ever been there?"

Sammy shook his head. "No, but I've seen *La Dolce Vita* at least twenty times." He gulped. "It was my father's favorite."

Dre suddenly pressed Sammy flush against his hard, broad chest. "Then Rome it is. I'm sure you're going to like it. I know some cool places there."

"We're going to travel demon-style?" Sammy couldn't keep the excitement out of his voice. Dre chuckled.

"Of course. I promised you. Remember?"

"You did."

They were silent for a few moments, staring into each other's eyes. Sammy noted that the crimson in Dre's gaze had faded and been replaced by black. It took all his willpower to stop staring into the depths in which he could easily lose himself.

"So, you were looking for a manga?"

Dre shook his head like a kitten that had just gotten wet. He clearly had been lost in his own world as well. When he started to smile, Sammy had butterflies fluttering in his belly.

"Yes. I was told you're the man to talk to."

With some difficulty, they let go of each other. Sammy straightened and gestured toward the desk where his computer sat.

"Then let's go over there and see what I can do for you."

Chapter Four

Dre was nervous. He didn't want to admit it, but there was no other explanation. Why else would he have changed his outfit three times already, still not satisfied with how he looked? He wanted to impress Sammy so badly that he almost didn't recognize himself.

"Hey, big brother, why are you having a staring match with the mirror?"

Barion was leaning in the door to Dre's bedroom. His brother had come over to his place when he'd heard about the date. Dre could understand. This was the first time in almost a hundred years that he was going on a date—and with a human to boot. After his last, disastrous attempt at a relationship, Dre had restricted himself to hookups, only to spare himself the pain of being cheated on. Why in the nine hells he'd thought trying to build a life with an incubus was a good idea, he couldn't tell. Back then, he'd been so in lust that he'd had trouble remembering his own name. Only finding his so-called partner in bed with not one, but two other demons had finally opened his eyes. He'd tossed the horny fucker out on his hot ass and spent the next year licking his wounds. Like Barion, Dre yearned for a stable relationship with somebody special.

Looking at his brother, Dre could see that Barion was dying of curiosity about who had managed to get him to date again, but Dre had kept the information about Sammy and the details about the date vague. He loved his brother with all his heart, but he had no intention of giving him a chance to ruin the date with one of his well-meant interferences that always ended in chaos. He and Sammy needed some time alone before Dre would even think about introducing him to any family members.

"I'm not sure if I should wear this shirt or..." He tugged at the black silk shirt he was wearing while looking for the dark red one he had tried on before.

Barion shook his head. "If I wouldn't know better, I'd say you're actually nervous, Dre. And that can't be. Can it?"

Dre didn't answer. Admitting to himself that this date meant more to him than any date he'd ever had was one thing. Telling his little brother was probably not wise.

"You *are* nervous! Dre, the charmer, is nervous about going out with a human. Wait!" Barion furrowed his forehead and the silver patterns on his skin seemed to glow. Where Dre was red, Barion was blue, but they both had the silver marks that announced them as royalty. The patterns on the other demons were either black or—if they were warriors—bronze. "Could he be—?"

"Don't even go there, Barion."

"But, Dre, this is important!" Barion pouted, which looked ridiculous on a male his size.

"I said don't go there. I'm having a date with a human I find interesting and whose scent I like. There's no need to get all excited."

"But—"

Dre shook his head. Barion was a romantic at heart and still dreamed of finding his fated mate one day. For demons, that was a bit more difficult than for other paranormals. Shifters recognized their mates by scent, as did vampires. Gargoyles needed to hear their mate's voice to know, and phoenixes reacted to the aura. They all knew instantly who their mate was. For demons, it was different. For one, it was rare for a demon to find his or her true mate. There were only two dozen couples or ménages who'd had such luck. And a demon couldn't tell immediately if somebody was their mate. They could find a person's scent intriguing, like Dre did Sammy's, but that didn't necessarily mean anything. It was a hint, nothing more. The only way Dre would know was when he bit Sammy during sex and his skin pattern developed on Sammy afterward. It was a sign that the body of the mate had undergone the necessary transformation to enable him or her to be a demon's companion. Since that transformation was rumored to be painful, Dre was in no hurry to bite Sammy—not to mention that Sammy would probably appreciate being told about the possible implications of sleeping with a demon.

"Even if he is my mate, this is our very first date. I don't want to overwhelm him. I just want him to have fun."

"So, it could be." The pure longing and hope in Barion's voice kept Dre from lashing out at his brother.

He understood how much his brother longed for a mate because he felt the same. He had just learned to deal with this yearning by ignoring it, which was unhealthy, as he well knew. But at least kept him from becoming depressed because his chances of finding his mate were slim to nonexistent. Sammy was like a ray of sunshine in a dark room, though Dre still refused to be too enthusiastic.

"Yes, it could be. But it's too soon to tell, and I don't want to get my hopes up. I'm going to enjoy this night, and if he wants to see me again, I'll work from there."

Barion sighed. "You're right. Sorry, Dre. I didn't mean to be a nag. It's just—"

"I understand. Really. And you will find your mate, Barion. I'm sure. Now what do you think? The red or the black shirt?"

"The black one. Brings out your eyes," Barion said after carefully assessing Dre. "You want to look your best when you take him to...?"

"Nice try, little brother. I'm so not going to tell you where I'm taking him. Perhaps afterward."

"That's just plain unfair. I promise that I won't do anything. I just want to know!" Barion whined.

Dre shook his head. "I know you. You promise me now, but the moment I'm gone, you'll start wondering, then you get impatient after five minutes of waiting. Then you can't hold back anymore and you follow me, and we both know what's going to happen then. No. I love you but *no*."

Before Barion could voice his protest, Dre closed the last button on his shirt, took his wallet and cut open time and space to step into Sammy's kitchen. Barion's high-pitched whine was the last thing he heard before he was greeted by a shriek and the sound of breaking glass.

"Jesus, Dre!" Sammy stood next to the kitchen counter with one hand clutched to his chest. The sweet smell of strawberry marmalade permeated the air. Dre glanced over the kitchen table and saw shards of glass and a red smudge on the floor.

"I'm so sorry, Sammy. I didn't mean to startle you."

Dre was contrite. What a terrible way to begin a date. Sammy rubbed his chest. He wore a white button-down with anthracite-color slacks that hugged his body just right. Dre couldn't wait to see Sammy from behind. He shook his head to get rid of his inappropriate thoughts when he realized why Sammy was still rooted to the spot like a statue. He was barefoot. Dre rushed over to him, careful not to step into the marmalade, and lifted Sammy out of harm's way. Before he let him down again, Sammy slung his arms around Dre's neck, which felt so good that Dre almost toppled over.

"Hi, Dre. It's good to see you."

Sammy's breathless voice was close to his ear. "And don't worry about the marmalade. It's store-bought and nowhere near as tasty as the one Mavis and Maribell make."

Dre chuckled, pressing Sammy closer to his body, unwilling to let him go. "Would I be in trouble if it had been one of their glasses?"

The answer came without hesitation. "Yes. Wasting their cooking is a sacrilege. You'll understand once you've tasted their cookies."

"I can't wait."

Sammy bent his torso back far enough to look into Dre's eyes. Their lips were so close that Dre thought he could feel the heat coming from Sammy. They both moved forward as if somebody was pulling invisible strings until their lips met in a chaste kiss that sent shudders down Dre's spine. Sammy gripped Dre's shoulders like a vise. He was panting.

"Hello, Dre."

"I think you already said that."

"Did I?"

"To be honest, I can't remember."

Silence fell around them while they kept on staring at each other. Sammy's weight felt pleasant in Dre's arms, and he knew he would never tire of his differently colored eyes. The one with the brown iris had flecks of gold that reminded Dre of amber. The blue one was not really blue on closer inspection, but a mixture of gray, a very light blue — like the sky in spring — and some faded green dots. *Fascinating and gorgeous.*

"I think you can let me down now."

Dre didn't like that idea, but he did as Sammy asked. Once Sammy's feet touched the floor again, he went for the kitchen door.

"Just let me get some shoes. Then I'm going to clean up this mess and we can leave."

Dre shook his head. "I've got a better idea. How about you get ready for our date while I clean up the mess, since I'm responsible for it — more or less."

Sammy looked at the mix of glittering shards and sticky red mass on the floor then back up to Dre.

"If you insist."

Dre grinned. "I insist. Now get your sexy ass out of here so I can impress you with my cleaning skills."

"You think my ass is sexy?"

Sammy sounded more incredulous than teasing, which told Dre he wasn't used to getting compliments. Well, Dre could definitely remedy that.

"Oh yes. Very sexy. It's one of the reasons I asked you on a date." He waggled his eyebrows for emphasis.

Sammy opened his eyes wide and clutched his chest in mock consternation.

"You only want me for my body!"

"I see we understand each other."

They both started laughing and Sammy turned back to the door. "No magic to clean up!"

Dre huffed. "Don't worry. A demon's magic is better suited to *create* a mess than to clean it up—though the color would fit."

Sammy gasped. "Dre!"

"Just kidding. Where do you keep your cleaning utensils?"

"Under the sink. I won't take long."

The slight frown on Sammy's forehead was too cute.

"Don't worry, Sammy. I got this."

"If you say so."

With one last glance, Sammy vanished through the door. Dre went to the sink to retrieve a cloth and some detergent. Careful to not get his clothes dirty, he bent down and started swiping up the marmalade and glass shards. The bigger ones he collected to go into the trash can, the smaller ones he washed down with the marmalade in the sink. He was just giving the floor one last swipe when Sammy returned with nice black boots and a light blue V-neck pullover to complete his outfit. He looked absolutely stunning.

"Wow, Sammy, you're so beautiful." Dre spoke with absolute conviction and the blush on Sammy's cheeks was the sweetest reward. "You're going to need a warm jacket. Even though it's pretty warm in Rome, the temperatures still drop during the night."

"Wait a moment and I'll get my coat."

Sammy bounced out of the kitchen again. Dre used the time to clean the cloth and hang it over the tap on the sink. Sammy rushed back in, now with a coat with a white and dark blue herringbone pattern dangling from his left arm.

"I'm so excited, Dre! Just to warn you, I've read up on all the trivia about Rome, and I so want to see the Colosseum." Sammy paused when he stood right in front of Dre, his two-colored eyes glinting happily. "Thank you for taking me, Dre."

Dre put his arm around Sammy's slim waist. He wasn't entirely sure where they stood regarding their relationship but he liked touching Sammy, and Sammy seemed to be on board if the embrace when he'd arrived had been any indication. Still, Dre decided to not rush things. His lips grazed Sammy's hair in a brief, chaste kiss.

"Thank you for agreeing to go with me." He leaned back a bit to look at Sammy. "And just for the record, I read up on Rome as well. We can have a little match about who knows more."

"Geez, competitive much? I like it. Challenge accepted."

They grinned at each other like madmen.

"So, what did you plan for tonight? Or is that a secret?"

Dre pulled Sammy closer again, enjoying how well the young man fit against his side. "No. We'll start at this little restaurant I know. After we have dinner, we'll take a stroll through the historic parts of Rome, get some gelato for dessert and see what tickles our interest. Are you a church kind of guy?"

Sammy shook his head. "No, not really. I mean, I do appreciate the art and everything, but what fascinates me most are the antic parts — the Colosseum, the Catacombs, the Forum Romanum."

"Splendid. A man after my own heart. This is going to be great. Now hold on."

Dre loved how tightly Sammy clung to him while he let one of his claws slide out to cut space and time. Traveling like this was second nature to him, but seeing how Sammy reacted to the tug when the seam opened, followed by being sucked into the darkness of nothing then being spit out at the destination, was highly entertaining. One day soon he would take Sammy hopping around the world.

"Wow, this is so surreal." Sammy looked around the small blind alley where they had reappeared. "It's nothing like traveling with the Tardis or like Stargate. It's much quicker and with less light effects. Why's there no sound? And are we really in Rome?"

Dre snickered. "No, it's nothing like *Dr. Who* or *Stargate*, but then again, we're not using wormholes and I don't have a multifunction screwdriver. But I think it would be possible to add some light effects, if you want to. It's all magic, after all. And yes, we're really in Rome. To be precise, we're in a little alleyway off Via Panisperna on Monti, which is just above the Roman Forum. We're going to have dinner here."

Dre held out his arm and Sammy took it without hesitation. The sun was about to set and the air was still pleasantly warm. They went out of the alleyway and around the corner of the brick building with the fading paint to the forefront, where a small blackboard sign announced that the restaurant was open. Dre held the door for Sammy as they entered the narrow hall with framed posters of old films hanging on the walls. Sammy tugged on Dre's shirt.

"Look, Dre! *La Dolce Vita!*" He pointed to one of the posters with Marcello Mastroianni and Anita Eckberg. "Oh, and it's signed!" Sammy stared at the poster with wide eyes. Dre smiled and let him look his fill before he gently tugged him toward the door that would lead them into the restaurant. It wasn't big—only eleven tables and a small bar in one of the corners. Cobblestones made the floor, as if the room were outside on a piazza, and the ceiling was vaulted, hinting at the age of the building. The restaurant was empty because Italians tended to eat rather late in the evening. At the other side of the room, a door leading to the kitchen opened. Dre smiled when he saw Zenobia, the current matriarch and owner of the restaurant, make her way toward them. He'd known her since the day she was born, and seeing her now, over seventy years later, was always bittersweet for Dre. The woman whose hair had once been as black as a raven's wing stretched out her hands to touch both Dre and Sammy.

"Dresalantion! How nice of you to come by. And you brought a guest?" Zenobia looked at Sammy. Dre had no doubt she already knew who his date was, but he played along.

"Zenobia, this is Sammy, my date. Sammy, this is Zenobia, the owner of this place and an old friend of mine."

Sammy took Zenobia's hand tentatively. His eyes went wide with shock when the old woman reached up, grabbed his nape and lowered his head to her meager height of barely five foot one. Her lips came close to Sammy's ear and Dre felt a surge of irrational jealousy. With his demon hearing—which wasn't as good as shifter or vampire hearing, but still way better than that of humans—he picked up what Zenobia whispered.

"Do not despair, *mio piccolo passero*, because hearts can be healed."

She pressed a kiss to Sammy's cheek, threw Dre a mischievous glance and took both their hands. "Follow me, *piccioncini*. I have the perfect table for you."

Zenobia led them to a small table for two in a corner that was partly obscured by one of the columns that held the ceiling. After Dre had seated Sammy, Zenobia clapped her hands. "Food will come." With that, she turned around, her black skirt billowing around her with a sound like a thousand bats taking flight. She was gone before either of them could utter a word. Sammy cleared his throat.

"I guess there's no menu?"

Dre shook his head. "No, never. The restaurant has no name, either. But the food is delicious."

Sammy smiled. If Zenobia's cryptic words had in any way flustered him, he didn't show it. "So, on a scale from one to ten, how paranormal is she?"

Dre chuckled, delighted by Sammy's wit. "What gave her away?"

"She knows your name." Sammy lifted his thumb. "She knew who I was. No, don't try to deny it. I know the signs." He lifted his index finger. "You heard what she said to me." His middle finger came up. "And lastly, she gives this crazy vibe I have come to associate with non-human beings." Four fingers waggled in front of Dre and he had to suppress the urge to grab Sammy's hand and kiss them, one after the other.

"Wow, I forgot I'm with an expert." Dre laughed. "You're right, of course. Zenobia comes from a long line of priestesses. She's human, but one with some very special talents."

"A witch?" Sammy looked suspicious. Since he was used to the company of witches, Dre could understand his reaction. Witches weren't always good news. They could be downright nasty if they wanted to, so he hastened to reassure Sammy.

"No, although it's similar. She's a high priestess to the mother goddess, who goes by many names – Gaia, Hecate, Morrigan, Danu, Isis. The list is long, as you know. Zenobia and her family have served the goddess in an unbroken line since before the first pyramids were built."

Dre couldn't help it. He loved how Sammy hung on his every word.

"If this is the kind of knowledge you're going to share tonight, then you've already won our challenge. This is fascinating. How long have you known them?"

"Zenobia's family? For about four hundred years. I met her ancestor Paxe when I first came to Rome. She already had the restaurant then, and the food was just as good."

Sammy raised a brow. "You're kind of an uber-regular, aren't you?"

Dre chuckled. "You could say that."

Before Sammy could open his mouth again, a younger version of Zenobia approached their table with a carafe of wine and a jug of water. She smiled broadly at them.

"Good evening, Dresalantion, Sammy. I hope you enjoy your meal here."

The young woman put two clay mugs in front of each of them, filled two with water and two with the dark red wine before she bent slightly forward to ignite the thin white candle between them by blowing on it.

"Thank you, Aulina."

"My pleasure." She winked at them and left.

"That was Aulina, Zenobia's granddaughter."

"Beauty seems to run in that family."

"Not only beauty, as you've seen."

Dre picked up his clay mug with the wine. "To a wonderful date in the eternal city."

Sammy clinked his mug against Dre's. "Cheers."

They took a sip of their wine and Sammy's eyes widened. "This is good."

"Oh yeah. They know how to make good wine." Dre looked around before he leaned over the table, closer to Sammy, who had a curious glint in his eyes. "Rumor has it that the wine the Pope drinks during mass on Easter and Christmas comes from here as well."

Sammy's grin was so wide that Dre feared it would split his face in half.

"Stop giving the boy weird ideas." Zenobia had approached the table without them noticing her. She put plates in front of them, a basket with bruschetta slices and a small pot with a greenish spread. "All wine consumed during service is *the* wine. Everybody knows that." She patted Sammy's hand. "Enjoy your meal."

Dre and Sammy each got a slice of bread, which was still warm, covered it with the spread and took a bite. Sammy moaned.

"Mm-m. So good. What's in it?"

Dre licked his lips. The food was good, but Sammy's groans were even better.

"It's a mixture of ricotta cheese, olive oil, basil and garlic. One of my favorites."

"I can see why. I could bathe in this stuff." Sammy took another bite, making appreciative noises in the back of his throat that had Dre's libido burning. It got worse when Zenobia brought them the next course, linguine with artichokes and a lemon sauce that had Sammy moaning like somebody was licking his body from head to toe. Apparently, Sammy loved food. His reaction to the main course, *saltimbocca romana* with young potatoes, had Dre's cock straining against the zipper of his jeans, and after dessert, a panna cotta with strawberry and raspberry sauce, Dre knew he had made the right decision by bringing Sammy there. When they rose to leave, Zenobia took their hands again, murmuring something in a language they didn't understand. Once they were out of the door, Sammy looked at him.

"What was that?"

"A blessing. Zenobia likes you a lot. You're the first date I've brought here that she served personally."

Sammy halted so abruptly that it took Dre several steps before he realized his date was no longer at his side. With a questioning look, he turned around.

"You've brought others here?"

The drama in Sammy's voice might have alarmed Dre if it hadn't been for the mischievous glint in his eyes. He approached Sammy, slung his arms around his waist and pulled him close. "I hate to tell you that, *mo grah thu*, but you're the worst actor I've ever met."

Sammy leaned his upper body back to look into Dre's eyes. A faint blush tinged his cheeks, making Dre want to devour him right there on the street.

"I'm sorry. It's just— You're making me so nervous and I'm trying hard not to start with the verbal diarrhea, which isn't working so well, considering how you're looking at me right now. I want this to work so bad, because this is my first date ever and I'm wildly attracted to you and you probably don't want to go out with me ever again."

There was a wet sheen to Sammy's eyes now, a sheen Dre wanted gone. Slowly, he lifted his right hand and caressed Sammy's cheek. Sammy closed his eyes at the contact, whimpering softly. "Sammy, I don't want you to censor yourself. I already told you I'm a sucker for all kinds of knowledge myself, the geekier, the better. And I'm nervous, too. This is my first date in over a hundred years. My last relationship was terrible and ended in serious heartbreak on my side. So, as you can see, I carry my own baggage. And just for the record, I'm wildly attracted to you as well."

A tentative smile rose on Sammy's face. "You think we could work?"

The longing in Sammy's voice tore at Dre's heart, because it was so similar to his own. "Yes, *mo grah thu*, I think we could definitely work."

"What does '*mo grah thu*' mean?"

Dre smiled down at Sammy. "It's an endearment, meaning 'my love'."

"Oh." The blush on Sammy's cheeks deepened, then he grinned. "Mavis and Maribell are probably going to kill me, but I'm really enjoying my date with a demon."

Dre chuckled. "And it has just started."

He slung his arm around Sammy's shoulder and led him down the Monti toward the Roman Forum.

Chapter Five

Sammy couldn't believe it. He was on a date…in Rome…with a demon. No, not just with a demon, with the most gorgeous demon he could imagine. The food had been beyond delicious and Dre hadn't gotten fed up with his nervous ass, something Sammy had feared from the moment he'd dropped the glass with the marmalade. He knew Mavis and Maribell wouldn't have approved of this date, which was one of the reasons why he hadn't told them. The second reason was that this date was the first happy thing in a long time that belonged solely to him. After the death of his parents, all his happiness—with the exception of the bookstore—had been shared, because he just couldn't be happy on his own anymore. This thing between him and Dre, though… It made him giddy with joy and tremble in fear at the same time. Sammy just didn't know if he was strong enough to experience loss again, and with every second he spent in Dre's company, his conviction grew that losing the handsome demon would be devastating. There was also the fact of Dre's immortality, which doomed their relationship from the start. Sammy knew they weren't meant to be forever, but he sure wished for it. His rational mind told him to end it now, before he got too invested, but his heart— and his libido—voted against that. Sammy took a deep breath, decided to give his rational thought a holiday for the time being and concentrated on the gorgeous man next to him. The streets of Rome were bustling with a first onslaught of tourists and the natives going on the prowl for the evening. Many people looked at Dre with admiration and open hunger in their eyes. Sammy could relate. His date was fine, with his red skin, the silver tattoos that licked up his neck and the backs of his hands, his long, silver hair... Sammy frowned.

"Why aren't people running from you screaming? You don't look that human."

Dre pulled Sammy closer, a smile on his lips. "A mixture of selective ignorance and a dash of magic. People tend to ignore what can't possibly be, and those with more inquisitive or open minds are encouraged to forget the moment they realize something's odd about me."

"But I can see you clearly."

"Yes, you can." Dre sounded very pleased about that. "There are several reasons... First, you met me when I was summoned. It's hard to ignore such a blatant fact, even though you weren't awake when I appeared in the circle. Second, you're acquainted with the paranormal world. That takes the blinders off. Third, and most importantly, I think we're drawn to each other, which cancels out the magic."

"You like that." Sammy couldn't help a hint of pride creep into his voice. Dre must have picked up on it because he bent down to place a gentle kiss on Sammy's forehead.

"Yes, I like it a lot. Now, I believe we have a challenge going on. What do you know about the Roman Forum? And I want the lesser-known facts."

Sammy felt his brain switch gears. He loved a good geek challenge.

"Okay, where to start... I know! The reason the Roman Forum is on a deeper level than the rest of the city is because the Romans built on ruins, and throughout the centuries, a lot of debris has accumulated. Your turn."

Dre grinned. "The early days of the Forum go back as far as eight hundred BC, and the people who built it first drained the area to get rid of the grass."

"The excavation of the site took over a hundred years."

"There are many forums in Rome, but this one was the most important because the senate met here."

"Some of the temples aren't dedicated to gods but to people, because the Romans thought if they had a temple dedicated to them, they would become a deity."

"That's a good one. I wonder if Terry Pratchett knew about this when he wrote *Small Gods*."

Sammy chuckled. "I love how you can get from ancient Rome to *Discworld* in one sentence."

Dre bowed with a flourish. "I aim to please. Oh, and parts of the stones of the Roman Forum were used to build other places in the city and can be found in several churches and the Vatican."

"It's also one of the most popular sites in Rome visited by tourists," Sammy added.

"Okay, let's call this one a draw. Let's get our *gelato* and move on to the Catacombs."

"Aren't they closed at night?"

Dre smiled broadly at Sammy, which did strange things to his stomach and nether regions. "They are, but you're traveling with me."

Sammy giggled. "I can't wait to see them."

They got their *gelato* from a store that had about forty different flavors. It took them almost twenty minutes to decide what they wanted. Dre settled for pistachio and walnut, while Sammy went for the classics, vanilla and chocolate. The ice cream was scooped onto their cones with a spade, which made them look like little mountains. It was delicious and a bit messy. Sammy was just glad that the night air had a certain chill to it, because otherwise, the *gelato* would have melted before he could eat it.

"May I have a taste?" Dre looked at him with smoldering eyes. Sammy gulped and held his cone out, but Dre ignored the gesture and went for Sammy's lips instead. His hot tongue swept over the corner of Sammy's mouth. Sammy reacted instinctively by opening up. It was their first real kiss and Dre kept it simple, just sucked on Sammy's tongue for a moment before he righted himself again, a satisfied smile on his face. Sammy was glad, because if Dre had kept on kissing him, he might have come in his pants.

"Delicious." Dre licked his lips.

Sammy groaned. This was torture, albeit the good kind. And since this evening was already so perfect, he just went with the flow. He tried to scoop as much *gelato* as possible on his tongue, making sure Dre was watching, then tilted his head to him, offering his vanilla-smeared lips. "Want another taste?"

Now it was Dre's turn to groan. The demon bent back down. Almost in slow motion, Sammy could see

Dre's eyes turning crimson. He knew he should be alarmed. He knew Dre was dangerous. And yet all he felt was lust and a yearning from so deep down in his soul that he didn't want to think about it too much. Their lips met again, their tongues starting a slow, sensuous dance that had Sammy's entire body flushed with heat. They only stopped when they needed to come up for air. Panting, they stared at each other. Sammy caught a flash of fang from Dre and shuddered in anticipation. He wondered how it would feel, kissing Dre with his fangs out. The demon trembled under his light touch.

"We better get to the Catacombs *pronto*. The magic conceals only so much."

Sammy loved the rasping quality of Dre's voice, which assured him that the demon was as affected by their kiss as he was. They stumbled into the nearest alleyway, looking for a dark corner where nobody would see them vanishing. Dre pressed Sammy tightly against his body while he cut open time and space. They reappeared inside the Catacombs on the Appian Way, surrounded by darkness and a silence that was almost deafening. It was also colder underneath the surface. Sammy snuggled closer to Dre's body, enjoying the heat coming from the demon. Dre held out his right hand and a small ball of fire appeared on it. It hovered half a foot above them, shedding light and warmth. Once they had eaten their *gelato*, which took some time because of all the kisses they stole in between, they set out to explore. Sammy loved the way their shadows were dancing around the walls like creatures from another world. With Dre at his side, he didn't fear anything. They passed a long line of rectangular shapes hewn into the rock where the bodies of Jews and early Christians had been buried. The farther they went, the more elaborate those graves became, some of them with beautiful mosaics to honor the deceased. They stopped at one small grave where a child had been buried. Sammy felt sadness wash over him.

"I wonder what it was like, coming down here with the body of somebody you loved in your arms, putting them to rest among all the other who had gone before them."

Dre's arm tightened around him. "It was sad, I guess. Though you have to keep in mind that the early Christians were fierce in their belief. Perhaps they even felt some joy for the person who would, according to their lore, go to paradise."

Sammy leaned his head on Dre's muscular chest. "What's it like—being immortal, I mean?"

They started walking again, toward the exit of the Catacombs. "Boring, mostly. I'm only eight hundred years old, so I don't know that much about eternity yet, but from what my father has told me, it's hard not to get buried under the weight of the centuries."

"How old is your father?"

"Almost four thousand years. Back when he was born, things were more interesting, though. There were less humans, vast spaces where a demon could have fun—although fun in the olden days usually meant bloody war. Father is not unhappy that those days are over. Plus, he likes all the modern gadgets humanity has come up with. He's especially fond of his iPad and Netflix."

Sammy frowned. "I thought demons had their own realm. Why are you even here on Earth?"

Dre thought about this question for a moment, as if he were afraid to say something wrong. When he finally spoke, it was in a low tone, almost a whisper.

"Because we get lonely, just like everybody else. Too many demons in one place means war, usually sooner than later. We do get along with our family and some chosen friends, but all in all, we don't like each other too much. Father says this is a security mechanism to keep our kind from invading and conquering other realms. A demon army is pretty much unstoppable, and if we were united..." Dre shuddered. "Not a nice thought, believe me. Luckily, we can't keep the peace among ourselves long enough to even think about invasions. And the more sophisticated the human race becomes, the more fascinated we are. Humans are a great source of entertainment for us, and Father encourages demons actually living on Earth. It makes us less restless and easier to rule."

They reached the gate to the Catacombs. Dre took the lock that kept the chains around the bars together, shook it and, after it made a clacking sound, opened the gate. After they had passed, he closed it again. Hand in hand, they wandered along the Appian Way, enjoying the livelier silence of the night outside. In the Catacombs, even the air had been stifling, weighed down by the gravity of time, but out here, the sounds of nocturnal animals and the distant hum of Rome made for another, lighter mood. Sammy lifted Dre's hand to graze the knuckles with his lips.

"Are you restless?"

Dre stopped, turned sideways to face Sammy and kissed him softly.

"I was. As I said, I had a rough break-up about a hundred years ago. But tonight, with you, I feel more content than I can ever remember. This may sound terribly cheesy, I know, yet being here in Rome with you is like magic. The good kind."

Sammy tilted his head back to get another kiss. It was just a soft brushing of lips, nothing like the wild tango their tongues had danced before. Still, it was equally deep, not with passion, but with emotion.

"Yes, the very good kind. Do you have any other surprises for me?"

"Insatiable, are we?"

Sammy slapped Dre's chest. "Somehow, you bring it out in me. The greedy, bad side."

"And I like it just as much. It's already getting late, so I'll let you choose. We can go to the Fontana di Trevi, where Anita Eckberg took her bath, or to Ostia Antica. Your choice."

Sammy bit his lips. "You're not making this easy. Hm-m. Fontana di Trevi means going back into the city, where all the people are. I think I'm going to be extra greedy. I want you to myself."

"Ostia Antica it is." Dre smiled broadly. "I like the way you think. Besides, we can always come back for more of Rome." He slung his arms around Sammy's waist. "Let's go and I'll show you where the Ancient Romans took their shits."

When they appeared in the ruins of Ostia Antica, Dre could feel Sammy's body vibrating with excitement. Even though it was still early in the year and the typical Roman heat hadn't had time to permeate the old stone walls like it did every summer, the air was already heavy with the scents of sage and lavender. Crickets and other insects played an even nicer concert than on the Appian Way and the stars seemed to be closer here, where the city lights were far off. When Dre had first come to Ostia Antica, he'd fallen in love with the place, even though it had been a real dump four hundred years ago. Something about the old, derelict buildings with herbs and weeds growing between the stones, salamanders scurrying across the former floors of great buildings and butterflies dancing between the columns of temples dedicated to gods long gone spoke to him, drew him in. Sammy was reaching for his hand, and taking it came so naturally to Dre that it almost frightened him. Deep down, he'd already started to hope Sammy might the one, his destined mate. They just fit so perfectly together. He liked Sammy's nerdy nature, his social awkwardness that was gone the moment he felt in his element with a topic, his openness toward new people, the way he'd reacted to Dre, even though this was their first date. He looked down on the top of Sammy's head and marveled at how perfectly they fit together before he pressed their joined hands to his chest.

"Let's stroll around a bit. Can you see well enough, or should I get us a fireball?"

Sammy chuckled. "I'm tempted to say I need a fireball just to see it popping out of nowhere." He leaned against Dre. "I'm good. You can always conjure one when we get to the mosaics of Neptune's Bath."

"Oh, someone is back in challenge mode. Let's see, Ostia Antica most likely started out as a military base founded after the Romans beat the neighboring city Veji. There are some hints that it may have been built by Ancus Marcius, the fourth king of Rome in the seventh century BC, but historians aren't sure Ancus Marcius even lived, and the first mentions of Ostia Antica are from the fourth century BC."

"Good one, Dre. The name '*ostia*' comes from the Latin word *ostium,* which means river mouth and refers to the Tiber where it was built. It served as a harbor for trade, the only rival to Alexandria and Cartago, and to ship military. When the water of the Ostian Sea receded, two artificial harbor pools were built under the rulers Claudius, Nero and Trajan."

"I see you did your homework and I'm suitably impressed. But" — Dre lifted his index finger — "I bet no amount of reading prepared you for this." He tugged Sammy off the uneven road they'd just walked on toward one of the roofless houses where a kind of stone bank with holes the size of soup plates ran along the walls. "Tadah! A public *latrinae*. What do you say now?"

For a moment, Sammy seemed to be stunned. Then he started laughing. Between a cross of snorting and hiccups, he finally managed to say, "How utterly romantic. I don't know of any date in the history of dating where the couple went to see a public bathroom. This is hilarious!"

Dre did his best to look offended. "At least you can't accuse me of being boring or unimaginative. I put a lot of thought into this date."

Still chuckling, Sammy placed a hand on Dre's chest. His eyes burned with an emotion Dre hoped he didn't misinterpret. "You did. It's the best date I've ever had."

Dre raised a brow. "It's your first date."

"The best first date I ever had. The best date I could imagine, and believe me, I can imagine quite a lot. Tonight was everything I could have asked for and some more. Thank you, Dre."

Sammy went on tiptoe to press a kiss on Dre's lips. He still had to lower his head a bit for them to meet, though. When Sammy started to lean back, Dre slung his right hand around his nape to keep him in place. He loved how Sammy tasted, loved how soft his skin felt against his own, loved Sammy's scent that was now an intriguing mix of arousal and something more innocent. He wanted to plunder Sammy's mouth, wanted to drown in him, wanted to become one with him. Suddenly, Sammy moaned deeply against their locked lips and a wave of pure longing washed over Dre, followed by the coppery taste of blood. Dazedly, Dre realized it was Sammy's blood flooding his mouth. He reared back.

"Damn, Sammy! Are you hurt?"

Dre felt his fangs grow out fully and couldn't do anything against it. He stared at the thin red smear on Sammy's lips in horror.

"I'm sorry, Sammy, so sorry! I didn't mean to—"

Sammy lifted his right hand to his lips, dipped a drop with his index finger and stared at it in wonder. "So that's what it feels like." He sounded surprised.

"Baby, I—" Dre started patting his pockets for a tissue, only to come up empty. He felt sick to his stomach for hurting Sammy and guilty because he loved how Sammy tasted. Sammy reached for Dre's hand.

"It's okay, Dre. I wanted to know what it was like when you kissed me with your fangs." A broad smile appeared on his lips. "It's great."

"But, but you're bleeding!"

Sammy shrugged. "It's just a nick, nothing bad." He licked the blood from his lips. "Kiss me again."

Dre hesitated. He so wanted to comply, wanted to taste Sammy, feel him melt in his arms, but he didn't want to hurt him. Sammy closed the short distance between them, put his hands on Dre's chest and walked him backward until the back of his knees hit the edge of the *latrinae*. Dre sat down. He slung his hands around Sammy's waist when his date straddled his thighs. Their faces were so close that Dre could smell the hint of vanilla on Sammy's breath. His fangs were digging into his lips, making it difficult to speak.

"Shammy."

Sammy smiled. "The way I see it, kissing with your fangs out requires some getting used to. We need to train until we're proficient."

"Ownwy you can make kishing shound like a shore." Dre made a face. He sounded like a drunk. Sammy giggled.

"I'm sorry, Dre." He pressed light kisses on both of Dre's fangs. "It's just I can't remember when I last was so happy. Thank you for that. Now let's see if we can't work this out."

Sammy put his lips on the gap between Dre's, slowly dipping his tongue in. Dre moaned and opened. *This feels so good.* When Sammy started swirling his tongue around his left fang, Dre felt his cock pulsing in the same rhythm. He had never kissed with his fangs out before, but he found he liked it. Sammy did some more exploring, nibbled on Dre's lips and teeth, then swiped his tongue around in his mouth as if he were looking for something. When he felt confident enough that he wouldn't accidentally hurt Sammy again, Dre did some exploring of his own. He didn't know how long they kept on kissing. He just allowed himself to get lost in the wonderful sensations of having Sammy in his arms, tasting and feeling him, pulling him so close that it felt as if they were one. Only when Sammy started squirming in his arms did Dre loosen his hold.

"What's up?"

An adorable blush appeared on Sammy's cheeks. "I'm afraid I need to use the bathroom. Can you...you know, do your thing and transport me somewhere with a porcelain bowl?"

Dre was about to get his claws out to open time and space when he suddenly had an idea. "Number one or number two?"

"Huh?"

"Do you need to piss or take a shit?"

The blush deepened. "Number one."

Dre grinned. "Then we don't have to go anywhere." He made a sweeping gesture. "We're in a bathroom."

For a moment, Sammy seemed stunned. Then he started shaking his head vigorously. "Oh no. I'm not going to piss in an ancient monument. No chance."

"Why not? Granted, there's no water running below to transport it away, but it's just piss. The next rain will wash away whatever hasn't soaked into the ground. Don't you want to know what it feels like?"

Sammy hesitated. "I guess it would be like a living history experiment...sort of. Still, it feels wrong."

Dre smiled at Sammy encouragingly. "I can take you somewhere else if you really don't want..."

Sammy stared at the holes in the bench. "You need to wait outside."

Dre's face fell. "But I wanted to know what it's like," he whined.

"And I will tell you, but you won't stay here while I...I obey my biological needs. Whatever this thing between us is going to be, we're not yet at the stage where I don't care about matters of the bathroom. So out with you!"

Dre chuckled but obeyed. He stepped through the gap in the walls where the entrance had once been, and kept his back to Sammy. "Satisfied?"

"Promise you won't turn around."

Dre held up his pinkie finger. "Pinkie swear."

He got an almost hysterical laugh as an answer. "You're insane." Then Dre heard the rustling of clothes, the zing of a zipper being pulled down, a shriek when Sammy's naked ass connected with the cold stone — there would be no way he could hit the small hole accurately — then the trickling of fluid. Another rustling told Dre that Sammy was getting up and back into his pants.

"Can I come in?"

"Yes."

Dre turned around to go back into the *latrinae*. He found Sammy standing there with his eyes wide open. His hands were shaking at his sides.

"I can't believe I did that. I took a leak in an ancient building with my date listening. Oh my God, what have I done?"

Dre hurried to take Sammy in his arms. He sounded as if he needed it.

"You did a historical experiment, and if it's any consolation, I think the sound of you taking your clothes off is highly erotic."

Sammy looked up at him. Slowly, he opened and closed his eyes, reminding Dre of an owl. "I'm not sure if it's a good thing that you bring out my daring side. I've never done something like this before. Never. I'm the good boy, the silent nerd who reads books and doesn't get into any trouble. I do *not* piss into ancient toilets."

Dre raised a brow. "How was it?"

Sammy shuddered. "Exciting. Cool. Terrifying. And you listened!"

"So mostly it was good, wasn't it?"

"Yeah…mostly. I'm just not sure if I want to do it again."

"You don't have to. Let's stroll around a bit more until the adrenaline in your system wears off. Then I'll take you home."

Sammy didn't protest when Dre led him out of the *latrinae* and back onto the cobbled, weed-covered streets of Ostia Antica. They walked around for thirty more minutes, visiting the theater and the temples before Dre took them back into Sammy's kitchen.

"Thank you, Dre. It was a fantastic evening."

Sammy looked up into Dre's eyes, so sincere and beautiful. Dre simply had to lean down and kiss him again. And again.

"It was my pleasure. How about we do this again, tomorrow?"

"You want to go back to Rome?" Sammy sounded breathless and not at all taken aback by the idea of seeing Dre again in such a short time. One glance at the clock on Sammy's oven told Dre it was even the same day.

"We can do that, but I was thinking we could go skiing in Canada."

"I don't know how to ski." Sammy seemed a little dejected.

"Do you want to learn?"

"I'd love to!"

"Then Canada it is. Try to get some sleep. I'll be back here at nine, which gives you seven hours of sleep." Dre grinned broadly. Sammy groaned.

"I didn't even realize it was that late. Being with you makes time fly."

Dre bowed. "My pleasure."

He leaned in for one last kiss. After their lips disconnected, he opened time and space again. "Dress in something warm. We can get you snow gear in Canada once we're there."

Chapter Six

Sammy was humming softly while he arranged the assortment of cookies and muffins that he got every day from the small bakery around the corner in glass jars and under the antique cheese domes made from Murano glass he had found at a flea market in Helena. He had them in various forms, sizes and colors and they looked nice on the battered wood of the counter he had secured when an old bar at the other end of town had been taken down. It was Monday and he was in a splendid mood, even though the muscles in his thighs and calves still protested every time he tried to move too fast. As it had turned out, skiing was a strenuous sport, and the human body had muscle tissue everywhere, even on the shins. The tinkling of the chimes announced some early customers. Sammy groaned inwardly when he saw Declan and Troy sauntering into the shop, immaculately dressed in tailored suits with their Thermos cups at the ready.

"Why can't you guys make your own coffee?"

"Good morning to you, too, Sammy. And you know why. It needs your magic touch to make it perfect." Declan grinned, showing all his pearly white, a little-too-sharp teeth.

"Good morning, Declan, Troy. You're just too lazy to learn." Sammy grumbled without real conviction while he took their cups. "Are you going out of town?"

Declan made a face. "Yeah. Business trip. Hopefully we'll be back for the book club meeting on Wednesday."

"Mmm-hmm-m." Sammy started making Troy's café latte, using the button that would produce an extra-strong espresso. He reached for the bottle with fresh milk—he had a case delivered to the shop three times a week from one of the local organic farmers— when Troy's voice cut through his happy thoughts.

"So, a little bird told us you were abducted to serve as a sacrifice during a demon summoning last week."

Sammy groaned. "Wasn't it an *old* bird, rather than a little one?"

Declan and Troy both held up their hands in a defensive gesture. "Your words, buddy, not ours."

"Cowards." Sammy grinned.

"Yeah, whatever. Now, who do we have to kill?" Troy sounded way too enthusiastic about the prospect of eviscerating somebody. Sammy blamed it on the early hour and the fact they had to go on a trip. Werewolves were by definition territorial creatures, and the small town of Beaconville was Troy and Declan's home. Leaving it, if only temporary, didn't sit well with their wolves.

Sammy poured the espresso into the Thermos before he started foaming the milk. The loud hissing of the steam pipe gave him some time to think about his answer. While he mixed the espresso with the milk, carefully creating a thick layer of foam, just like Troy liked it, he started to speak.

"If you know about the abduction, you also know about who saved me and that I have no clue who took me. What are you really here for, besides my delicious coffee?"

The two huge alphas had the decency to blush when Sammy turned around to set Troy's Thermos down before he took Declan's.

"Mavis and Maribell wanted us to talk to you. And just for the record, I'm not sure if they wanted us to explain to you the finer points and dangers of gay sex with a paranormal or to talk you out of it." Declan grinned a bit sheepishly.

"Why would you want to explain the finer points of sex to me? I never mentioned to Mavis I was attracted to Dre."

"But you are. And you've already been on a date with him." Troy shook his head as if Sammy were a child who had tried to hide something from the parents.

"How do you know that?"

The two werewolves touched their noses. Declan sounded matter-of-factly. "You reek of demon pheromones. Somebody's been all over you. *And* you haven't lost that little smile on your lips even once since we came in here."

Sammy lifted his arm and sniffed. All he could smell was the faint lemon scent of his soap. "I showered."

"So you don't deny it." Troy had smugness written all over his face. Sammy sighed.

"No, I don't deny it. In fact, Dre came shortly after Mavis had left and he asked me on a date. On Friday, we had dinner in Rome and visited Ostia Antica. On Saturday, he took me skiing in Canada, and yesterday we had a picnic in Machu Picchu. Dre is so nice to me, and we have a lot in common."

The two alphas looked at each other. Troy sighed dramatically. "Guess we're too late for the 'keep your hands off demons' speech. Sounds like Sammy's mysterious suitor is pulling out all the stops."

Declan nodded. An adventurous gleam entered his eyes, one Sammy didn't like in the least. "Then we better do the sex speech." He turned to Sammy, a serious expression on his face that could have fooled Sammy if it hadn't been for the tell-tale twitching of Troy's lips. Sammy slapped his hands over his ears.

"I don't want to hear it. In fact, I can't hear a word you're saying. La-la-la!"

Declan reached over the counter to pry Sammy's hands form his ears. "Oh, you will listen, young man. I'm not going to risk the wrath of the witches when they find out you weren't sufficiently prepared for your sexual adventures with a demon."

"How do they even know? I haven't told them on purpose," Sammy whined. The prospect of all his friends meddling in his—whatever he had with Dre, hopefully a relationship—was a nightmare.

"They're witches, man. We don't ask, and we certainly don't tell. Back to you. Have you kissed with your demon already? Because doing the tongue-tango with fangs can be tricky."

Sammy felt heat crawling from his neck up to his ears when he remembered their intense training sessions. He couldn't believe he was having this conversation. Why couldn't the floor open up and swallow Declan and Troy? While he tried to hide his embarrassment, Sammy started with Declan's coffee.

"Don't you worry. We have the fangs sorted out."

Both alphas whistled. "That's what, second base all covered?" Declan asked Troy. Sammy decided to ignore them. He pushed the button for a double espresso and listened to the calming sound of coffee beans being grounded. Unfortunately, Declan and Troy were like toddlers who demanded his undivided attention. "Are you prepared for third base? And fourth?"

Sammy poured the remaining milk foam into Declan's Thermos. "I'm not talking about bases with you."

"Then how about cocks?" As crude as the words were, Sammy could hear the laughter in Troy's voice.

"We're not going to talk about cocks either." Sammy turned to hand Declan his coffee. "You two are taking your caffeine out of my shop without further mentioning of cocks or bases. If Mavis and Maribell ask, I promise to cover for you, but talking about this with you two just seems wrong. Hell, it seems wrong talking about it at all. And I'm not completely clueless, you know."

The two alphas shared a look. Troy cleared his throat. "We don't think you're clueless, Sammy. It's just that being with a paranormal is challenging enough. Make that paranormal a demon and it's even worse. I'm sorry if we're making you uncomfortable." Declan snorted, and Troy rolled his eyes. "Fine, I'm not sorry. Happy now?" he asked, turning to Declan, who just nodded. "Sammy, you have to believe us. We want you to be happy and, above all, we want you to be safe. Doing the nasty with a demon requires serious preparation, because those guys are hung like horses. You need to stretch yourself properly if you don't want it to hurt and — "

"La, la, la! I can't hear you!" Sammy was practically screaming. "Go on, shoo. You have a business trip. Don't let me detain you." He stepped around the counter and started shoving the laughing alphas out of the shop. When the shop door closed, Sammy breathed a sigh of relief. He knew Troy and Declan meant well, but he wasn't ready to discuss his sex life with them, especially not the technical details that he hadn't completely thought through on his own yet. He felt insanely attracted to Dre, and just kissing him had Sammy hard to the point of pain. He also knew enough about gay sex to realize that the baseball bat he'd felt through Dre's trousers would be a challenge, mildly put.

Maybe it was a good idea to do some experimenting on his own, to find out how much he could take. Apart from regular masturbating as was normal for a healthy young male, Sammy had little-to-no experience with sex when a second person was involved. He wondered if there were books about sex with paranormals and where he could find one. If things with Dre kept progressing like they were, it wouldn't be long until their heavy make-out sessions would turn into something more. The mere thought had Sammy's heart beating faster. He wanted this — not only the sex or the unbelievably hot and funny dates. He wanted Dre.

Filled with new determination, Sammy made himself a cup of hot chocolate before he went to his laptop.

* * * *

"Hi, stranger. Haven't seen you in days." Barion sounded overly cheerful when he entered Dre's kitchen. He paused and started sniffing the air for dramatic effect. "Somebody's quite excited."

Dre flipped his brother off while taking another sip of his morning tea, a blend of herbs from the demon realm that could wake the dead. Dre liked it a lot. He was still too ecstatic about the three dates he'd had with Sammy on the weekend to let his brother get to him. Sammy was so sweet, so hot, so wonderful. Dre felt his heart and cock swell just thinking about the human.

"I had a great weekend."

Barion went over to the cupboard, got a mug and poured himself some of Dre's tea. He sniffed it once with a disgusted expression before he found the sugar and dumped four spoonsful into it. Stirring the concoction, he went over to the table where Dre was sitting.

"Come on, big brother. Don't leave me hanging like that. Give me details!"

"He's so sweet, Barion. We went to Rome on Friday. Had dinner at Zenobia's place, then went to see the Roman Forum, the Catacombs and Ostia Antica. Saturday, I took him skiing in Canada. You should have seen him. Even though he has zero talent, he tried the entire day until he was able to glide down one of the beginner's hills. His face was all flushed from the cold, his cute nose peeking out from between the scarf and the woolen hat. I almost ravished him right on the slope. Yesterday we had a picnic in Machu Picchu. We prepared it together in his kitchen. He knows how to make killer sandwiches."

"Brother, I think you've got it bad. Even when you were with he-whose-balls-shall-rot-and-fall-off, you weren't so excited. You're practically glowing. When will you introduce him?"

"Not before I have thoroughly prepared him for the occasion. I love you, Barion, and I know you mean well, but I don't want to spook Sammy. You can be a bit over-eager sometimes."

Barion pouted. "Where's the trust, bro?"

"I trust you with many things, little brother. You know that. My potential mate is not among them." There, he'd said it, his deepest hope that kept surfacing from the dark place inside him where he'd buried it over a hundred years ago.

Barion clapped his hands. "You think he's the one?"

Before Dre could answer, his smartphone buzzed, telling him he had a WhatsApp message. Absentmindedly he swiped the screen to see what it was. A huge smile spread his lips when he realized that it came from Sammy.

Miss U. Looking forward to the weekend.

Attached was a link to a *National Geographic* article about an important Viking warrior who had turned out to be female. Dre sent a heart, a kissing emoji and two clashing swords back. He was so looking forward to their trip to Sweden on Saturday. For Friday, they had planned to cook together in Sammy's apartment.

"Is that from Sammy?" Barion had tiptoed closer to get a look at the screen of Dre's smartphone. "Wow, you're already sending him hearts? You move fast, bro."

"Get away from me, you menace. This is none of your business."

Dre turned his bulky body to keep Barion from taking another peek, which was pretty useless, since his brother used his time-bending skills to keep on reading.

"What's this about a female warrior?" Barion grew out one of his claws and pressed the link Sammy had sent. Since demon fingers were too big to handle the screens of smartphones, all of them used their claws to operate them. Who would have thought this lethal part of demon anatomy would find a peaceful use one day? Dre was sure this was Fate's way of getting a good laugh. The website opened, showing a picture of a woman with blonde hair, dressed in leather mail reinforced with steel. The headline read *Famous Viking Warrior Was a Woman, DNA Reveals*.

"Why is your date sending you a link about a Viking warrior?"

Dre grinned broadly. "Because we're going to visit famous Viking sites in Sweden on Saturday. And Birka, where this warrior was found, is one of our stops."

"Aren't there guides who can tell you all about it? Why research it yourself?"

"Because Sammy and I have this little challenge going. Who's able to gather more detailed information about the places we visit. Rome was a draw. I aced Canada, because Sammy didn't know a lot about snow. He wiped the floor with me regarding Machu Picchu. There's little he doesn't know about the Incas and their culture. We're both well-versed when it comes to Viking culture, and I can't wait to see what he has in store. This link is to tell me that I better gear up."

Barion just stared at Dre open-mouthed. Unlike Dre, he was more interested in the kind of fun one could have in a disco or bar. That Dre and Sammy considered reading up on an old culture as an entertaining way to spend their time was hard for Barion to understand.

"I think you really have found your mate. I'd never have thought there would be somebody who could match your level of oddity."

As much as Dre wanted to tell himself that this could just be a coincidence, Barion's words fanned the flames of hope in his chest. He could easily see himself spending the rest of eternity with Sammy, and if Sammy wasn't the one, Dre didn't want to find out how he would feel when he found his fated mate. He and Sammy just felt so right together, so perfect. Talking about Sammy woke the need in Dre to visit him. He closed the website and rose from his chair.

"I'm out, Barion. You can, of course, stay here, though I don't know when I'll be back."

Barion raised a brow. "Booty call?"

Dre refused to react to the teasing tone.

"Lunch with my boyfriend."

"Does he know you're coming?"

"No. But I'm going to make a short detour to Amsterdam to get him apple pancakes, so I'm sure I'll be welcome."

Dre winked at Barion and left.

* * * *

Sammy was engrossed with his e-reader when somebody cleared their throat. Startled, he shot out of the leather couch, almost dropping his reading device to the floor. After narrowly catching it, he turned around to see Dre standing next to the couch with an insulated box in his hands.

"Hi, Sammy. I thought we could have lunch together."

Sammy placed his e-reader on the table with Smaug and Drogon, making sure it was switched off. No way did he want Dre to see what he'd been reading. He would probably die of embarrassment. *The Guide to Successful and Satisfying Sex with a Paranormal* was so scorching hot and bluntly accurate that it had Sammy's body swinging from painfully aroused to completely shocked, like a metronome set on four quarters. And he had only read the foreword and the first chapter about common terminology so far. What would happen once he got to the actual instructions, he didn't know. His e-reader would probably combust. To hide his nervousness, he pointed at the box in Dre's hands.

"What's in there?"

Dre lifted the box. "Fresh apple pancakes from this quaint little café in Amsterdam. Want to try them?"

Sammy perked up. "I love pancakes! Put them down here. I'll get us plates and something to drink. What do you want?"

"I'm fine with whatever you're having."

"Peppermint tea with honey it is."

Sammy filled two mugs with hot water from the coffeemaker, placed two pyramid bags with peppermint leaves into them, put them together with two spoons, their plates and a pot of honey on one of his trays and brought them over to the lounging area. Dre was sitting on the leather couch, caressing the material with his fingers.

"This is a very nice couch, Sammy. And I love the table." Dre pointed to Drogon and Smaug.

"I found all the pieces on flea markets. Working on them was fun."

Sammy placed one of the mugs in front of Dre. Then he turned to the insulated box. "Can I just open it?"

Dre chuckled. "Sure. The pancakes don't bite."

Sammy rolled his eyes. "You're so funny." He took the lid off the box and gasped. "Dre, those aren't pancakes! Those are wheels! I've never seen anything this big."

"Those are traditional pancakes, as they're made in Holland. As you can see, they're a lot bigger and thicker than the ones we have in the US. They're also not as thin as French *crepes* or even German *Pfannkuchen*, which both are traditionally filled with either sweet or hearty things then rolled or folded. The pancakes, or *Pannenkoeken*, you see here are quite thick and the filling, in this case the apple slices, are placed on the dough while it still warms in the pan. There are also differences in the consistency and ingredients of the dough. *Crepes* are traditionally made with butter, milk, eggs and flour, while *Pfannkuchen* consist only of milk, eggs, flour and mineral water to make the dough fluffier. *Pannenkoeken* have yeast, butter, milk, eggs and flour in them. As you can see, the basic idea is the same, while the conducting varies. All kinds are delicious, though."

Sammy looked at Dre wide-eyed. He felt heat creeping up his neck to fill his cheeks. Dre was so damn sexy when he recited trivial facts. Before his natural shyness could get the better of him, he blurted out, "I think I'm falling in love with you."

Dre had just leaned forward to slice the pancake in half and froze midway over the insulated box, the knife poised above their lunch. Very slowly, he lifted his head. For a brief moment, Sammy feared he'd see rejection or disgust in Dre's eyes, although his logic told him that wasn't possible after the great weekend they'd had. When he finally met Dre's gaze, he saw that Dre's eyes had turned completely red and his fangs were poking over his lower lip. Sammy was just glad it was a slow Monday and the shop was empty.

"You can't say things like that, Sammy. You're killing me here. Do you have any idea how hard it is for me to keep my hands to myself? And you go and tell me what I've been longing to hear ever since Ostia Antica."

Dre straightened himself and put the knife down before he reached for Sammy to pull him into a tight embrace. "I think I love you, too, Sammy, even though it's still early days for us. And I want you so bad... So bad."

Sammy leaned into Dre's warm body, inhaled his delicious scent that was mixed with a hint of cinnamon and apples from the pancakes, and it must have been that heady blend that had him talking before his brain could intervene.

"We can't yet. I'm only through chapter one." The moment the words were out, Sammy bit his tongue, but it was too late. Dre pushed him back a little, a confused expression on his face.

"Chapter one?"

"Forget I said anything. Forget I even opened my mouth. Let's get back to cuddling and perhaps we can feed each other the pancakes? Before they get cold?"

"The pancakes are just as good cold as warm, and I'd love to feed them to you, but first, I want to know about that ominous chapter. What have you been up to, Sammy?"

"I'd rather not talk about it." Sammy was sure his skin had now the color of a ripe tomato.

"Now you're making me curious. Sammy, please, I need to know. We just declared our love to each other, which, by the way, was a lot less awkward than we both feared, if I may remind you of one of our first discussions."

"That was about finding out if we wanted to have a date, Dre. And awkward wouldn't even begin to describe the mood if I had to tell you what I've been reading."

Dre pulled Sammy back to his massive chest and kissed him on the forehead. "Come on, *mo grah thu*. Tell me."

Sammy shivered at the endearment. "You're not playing fair."

"Please!"

Sammy huffed. "Fine. But I warned you. And just FYI... If you so much as lift the corners of your mouth, I'm never going to forgive you."

Dre held up his hands in surrender. "I promise to behave."

Dre watched as Sammy turned back to the table where he had placed his e-reader. He couldn't believe it. Sammy had said he loved him. Well, that he thought he loved him, but that was just as good in Dre's book. Now he wondered what had Sammy so flustered. Sammy came back, switching the e-reader on. When he held the display to Dre's eyes, it took a moment for him to understand.

"You're reading *The Guide to Successful and Satisfying Sex with a Paranormal*?"

"You know the book?"

Sammy was beet-red, and if Dre's skin hadn't been red naturally, he would have blushed as well, though he did feel heat infusing his cheeks.

"Uhm, you know, it's a great book. Very detailed. With information that's not always easy to come by…" Dre knew he was blabbering. "You were right. This is beyond awkward."

Sammy arched a brow. "Believe it or not, I'm already feeling a little better about it. Why did *you* read it?"

"Do you remember when I told you about the bad break-up I had?"

Sammy nodded.

"I was with an incubus back then. When I realized our relationship was going down the drain, I tried to salvage it. I thought it would maybe help to surprise him with some new techniques in bed. Contrary to what you might think, I'm not that experienced when it comes to sex. He was an incubus, so I figured I was somehow lacking in that department." Dre sighed. "If I had paid the chapter about incubi more attention than just the obvious pointers about sex, I'd have spared myself a world of hurt."

"Oh, Dre, I'm so sorry." Sammy cupped Dre's face with both his hands, pulling him down for a gentle kiss. "He was an idiot to let you go. Any man who can recognize a quote from *Speed* and play *Halo* is a definite catch. Add your ability to take your date to places most people never get to see, not to mention your incredible good looks that hide the sweetest person I've ever met, and I'm grateful you haven't been taken before I met you."

Dre took a deep kiss from Sammy, too moved to answer him right away. "You say the sweetest things, *mo grah thu*. How about we eat the pancakes now and talk about why exactly you felt the need to read about sex with a paranormal." He waggled his eyebrows suggestively. Sammy slapped him on his biceps.

"Now it's awkward again…and embarrassing. As if you don't know why I was reading up on it."

"Well, what's better than putting a theory to the test? I, for my part, can't wait."

Sammy groaned. "Now I don't know how to keep my hands off you."

They both laughed and fell down on the couch. Dre reached for the box to retrieve their pancakes.

"I guess the peppermint tea is very well steeped now."

Sammy giggled. "The great thing about peppermint tea is that it's still delicious with the right amount of honey added."

"Isn't that a universal truth. Okay, open up for your first taste of *Pannekoeken*."

"I love it when you go all Archie Leach on me."

Dre arched his eyebrows. "If I keep saying sweet nonsense in a foreign language, does that mean we can move this to the bedroom?" he asked teasingly while he put the first piece of pancake in Sammy's mouth. Sammy started coughing.

"Dre!" He chewed twice before swallowing the bite. "Now I will forever associate apple pancakes with sex…or talk about sex. I'm not sure. Definitely not what something so delicious deserves."

"Isn't sex delicious as well?"

"You know what I mean. And I told you, I'm not ready yet. Remember…only the first chapter."

Dre forked another piece of pancake and put it in front of Sammy's mouth. "Okay, how about we read it together? That way I can intervene immediately if things are inaccurate."

"I thought this book was so good?"

Dre loved how Sammy kept his wits, even when the topic was difficult for him. "It is. Just in case... I never read the chapter about demons, you know."

Sammy sighed. "Fine, we read it together. And if I die of embarrassment, it's your fault."

Dre couldn't help himself. He kissed Sammy deeply, tasting the sugar, cinnamon and apples on his lips and underneath the by-now-familiar flavor that was all Sammy. The rest of their lunch break was spent with kissing and feeding each other the pancakes. Around two, people started flocking into the shop and Sammy got busy. Dre made a quick trip to his cottage to get his copy of *Corum*, found Barion had left without putting his tea mug away—which would have annoyed Dre more if he hadn't been in a hurry to get back to Sammy—and made himself comfortable on the leather couch after coming back to the book shop. He didn't get far, because he spent most of his time watching Sammy interact with his customers, most of whom seemed to be regulars. At half past five, the shop was empty again. Dre had just gotten up to go give Sammy a kiss and ask him if he needed help, when the chimes announced another visitor. Dre didn't need to turn around to know that trouble had just entered.

Chapter Seven

Sammy couldn't suppress a groan when he saw Mavis and Maribell enter the shop. They were dressed in their finest grandmother gear — all flowery aprons, knee-length dresses and their knitting baskets with the needles sticking out like a threat. Maribell wore a white bowler hat with a yellow floral print on it, while Mavis had opted for a church bowler in bright orange with a huge white silk rose at the side. It was their equivalent of armor.

As soon as they were through the door, their piercing gazes homed in on Dre, who must have felt the shift in the force, because he sidled toward the counter where Sammy was standing.

"Am I in trouble?" Dre mouthed.

Sammy shrugged. "I don't know. Either you, me — or both of us."

He wanted to say more, but Mavis and Maribell were already at the counter, smiling very sweetly at them. "Sammy, my dear, do introduce us to your friend here."

Mavis sounded like a noble lady who had just found the gardener sitting in her favorite seat with his dirty boots propped against the white tablecloth. Sammy swallowed nervously.

"Uhm, Mavis, Maribell, this is Dre, my…uhm, boyfriend."

Sammy saw Dre's face light up at his words and that helped him bear the strict looks he got from the witches.

"Well, Dre" — Maribell put more emphasis on the name than was strictly necessary — "as Sammy's friends and guardians in the paranormal world, we do have to ask you about your intentions with our boy." She gestured toward the couches. "Why don't we sit down and have a little chat?" Somehow, it didn't sound like a question.

Dre shot Sammy a pleading look. And even though Sammy would have loved nothing more than to go hide behind his coffeemaker, he took Dre's hand and led him back to the leather couch, knowing Mavis and Maribell preferred the one with the crocheted cover. They were in this together. Abandoning his boyfriend at the first sight of trouble was not how he wanted their relationship to start. When they were all seated, Sammy tried to smile at the witches in hopes of deflecting their wrath a little. "Can I get you something to drink? I think I have some muffins left, too. Are you hungry?"

"No, dear. Don't try to distract us. We're here to determine if Dre is right for you." Mavis let her gaze roam over Dre's muscular body and how it towered over Sammy's smaller form on the couch. Without thinking, Sammy leaned into Dre, taking comfort in his warmth, no longer sure who was protecting who. "He definitely passes when it comes to looks. Well done, Sammy."

Sammy wondered if the blush on his cheeks would become permanent, as often as it had happened to him during the last days. "Dre is right here, Mavis."

"We know, dear." Maribell smiled her best grandmother smile, the one that always had Sammy on edge because it meant trouble. "Now, Dre, what do you want from Sammy?"

Dre's hand settled on Sammy's nape before the demon started to talk.

"Sammy is very important to me. We just figured out we're in love, and I want to see where that leads. Both of us do, actually."

Dre locked gazes with Maribell, and from the strange way he had phrased his answer, Sammy got the impression that he was telling the witches something he didn't want Sammy to know. Mavis' and Maribell's reactions didn't help to ease his suspicions. They stared at Dre intently, then at each other, then at Dre again.

"Are you sure?" Mavis sounded tentative.

"As sure as a demon can be. I assume you know what it's like for my kind."

The witches nodded. Sammy knew he was missing something important, and he didn't like it. He wasn't a child, just a human.

"What aren't you telling me, Dre? Mavis? Maribell?"

The three had the decency to look guilty. "It's not our place to tell you, Sammy. This is between you and Dre," Maribell said soothingly.

Sammy arched an eyebrow. "Correct me if I'm wrong, but you're here to chew Dre out because you think he's not good for me. Why are you suddenly on his side?" He looked at Dre. "What can't you tell me?"

Dre sighed and took Sammy's hands in his. "It's not that I can't or don't want to tell you, *mo grah thu*. It's just that I think it's too soon. Today is only our fourth date and I don't want to overwhelm or burden you."

Sammy stared at Dre with his mouth hanging open. "I appreciate that. I really do. But I'd appreciate it even more if you'd tell me what's going on. I know we still have a lot to find out about each other. Hell, I don't even know if you have siblings or what your favorite color is. All I know is that I like you, a lot—enough to call it love, even though I've never been in love before. It hurts, Dre, when you're keeping things from me." With an angry gesture, Sammy wiped away the tears threatening to spill over. He didn't know why he'd become so emotional all of a sudden, probably because this was all new to him. Under the watchful eyes of the witches, Dre kissed Sammy's tears away.

"I could never hurt you, *mo grah thu*. Never. It's just that I'm so afraid myself. You see, demons very rarely find their fated mates. I've been hoping to meet mine since I was old enough to understand the concept. The problem is that demons can only know for sure about their mate when they have sex and bite the person. I think you can see why I didn't want to put additional pressure on you. It's bad enough that I'm pressuring myself. I so want you to be the one, my forever, and I'm terrified what it means for us if you aren't."

Sammy realized he had been gripping Dre's shirt harder and harder while the demon spoke. The thoughts whirled around in his head, too fast to grasp one of them for closer examination. Dre thought they could be true mates. Sammy knew how sacred that concept was for paranormals. Dre was afraid to find out they weren't. It was similar to Sammy's fear of falling in love with somebody who would inevitably leave him because he was mortal. Even though they were a demon and a human, their fears and hopes were the same. The thought gave Sammy hope.

"What happens if you bite me and I'm your mate?"

Dre glanced briefly at the witches. "Maybe we should discuss this matter in private?"

Mavis and Maribell shook their heads vehemently. They had been watching their exchange with gleaming eyes. "Are you out of your mind, dear? I can't remember when we last had this much fun outside the bedroom. Go on. Don't mind us." Mavis snuggled up to Maribell as if they were in a cinema, watching a film. Sammy shot them a dirty look that they conveniently ignored.

"I guess that's what you get for being friends with witches." Dre chuckled lightly before he turned serious again. "When I bite you during sex, I inject a venom into you. It's not deadly or anything, so don't worry. It only reacts to my true mate. If you are the one, the venom will spread in your body and start to change it so it becomes compatible to mine. You will get the same tattoos I have on my body, as the outward sign that you belong to me."

"Why isn't my body already compatible to yours if I'm your true mate?" Sammy was puzzled. Dre opened his mouth, clearly not sure what to say, when Maribell chimed in.

"When you have sex with a demon, things tend to get heated in the truest sense of the word. They are the children of fire, after all. Usually, demons can control it and have normal sex without burning their partners from the inside out, but not when they are with their fated mate. That's why your body needs to change. It has to be made fireproof. Just imagine the fun you could have!" Maribell grinned broadly, looking like a young woman again.

Sammy hid his face in Dre's chest. "Can't you make them go away?"

Dre's chest rumbled with laughter under Sammy's cheek. "They're your friends. And they're right." He caressed Sammy's hair. "We don't have to rush, *mo grah thu*. Let's go on our dates this weekend. Let's read the book together. We can experiment, have some fun. And when we both feel the time is right, I can give you my bite. I'd be more than honored if you'd go on this journey with me."

"Of course I will, Dre. Of course I will. I just need some time to think about it all. It's a lot to take in."

"Yes, think about it, Sammy. And while you think, have fun with your demon boyfriend. You have our blessing." Mavis leaned over the table to pat Sammy's arm. "I guess we won't need those spells now." She pulled the knitting needles and knitwork from her basket to reveal an assortment of glowing orbs at the bottom, neatly stacked in what appeared to be two egg cartons. Maribell sighed.

"What a waste. They were good curses." She blew on the orbs and they vanished.

"You were ready to fight me over Sammy?" Dre sounded surprised.

"Of course we were, dear. Sammy is family to us...kin. We would never allow any harm to come to him." Mavis winked at Sammy, whose throat constricted. He was still loved. Even though he had lost his parents, he had managed to find a new family, a family willing to protect him, even against a superior enemy.

"Thank you," he croaked, which earned him another pat on the arm.

"We're on our way, dears. You surely have things to discuss." Mavis kissed Sammy on the cheek before she motioned Dre to lower his head so she could do the same to him. "Have a nice evening. And be prepared to be interrogated again during the book club meeting. The others love Sammy just as much as we do."

After Maribell had kissed them both as well, the witches left the shop. Not in the mood to deal with another customer, Sammy closed the door, even though he still had about thirty minutes until official closing time. From where he was leaning on the door, he stared at Dre.

"Wow."

"Yeah. Wow. We survived the inquisition."

"That too. I think I need some sugar." Sammy went for the counter where the muffins were stacked. He felt Dre's gaze on his back.

"Do you want me to leave, Sammy?"

"What? No. No! It's just... You know, I've been thinking about us together, about the long-term, how it would play out with you being immortal and me being mortal. I had some very sad *Lord of the Rings* associations in my head. Then you come along and tell me there's a chance I could be yours forever. I know how fast paranormals move when it comes to their fated mates."

"You mean, things just got real?"

Sammy put the blueberry muffin down that he had taken from the tray. "Very real. Don't get me wrong... If I *am* your mate, I'd be thrilled, though there are a few doors closing that I wouldn't want to."

Sammy looked at Dre and saw the understanding in the demon's eyes. Immortality meant he would never see his parents again. "And if I'm not your mate, I would have to live with the heartbreak of letting you go one day."

"I would never leave you, *mo grah thu*. Never." The absolute conviction in Dre's voice reassured Sammy.

"I know. But it wouldn't be fair to you if you had to stay with an old man, waiting for his death. Damn, I can't even imagine it without getting all worked up. I'm a mess!"

Dre stepped forward and took Sammy in his arms. "Then don't imagine it. Our story has just begun, and even though we might not have all the time in the world, we do have some of it. Let's enjoy our dating phase without worrying about the future. We can go slow, get to know each other better. And when we're both ready, I can give you my bite."

Sammy clung to Dre and buried his face in the hard chest. "You're aware that I'm only going to fall harder for you the longer we know each other?"

"I'm counting on it, *mo grah thu*. Now stop overthinking this. It's enough if I do it. Tell me how can I help you with closing the shop?"

Sammy straightened and looked around. "Actually, it's not too bad today. How about you put the pastries into the fridge in my office while I clean the coffeemaker. After that, I usually do a quick sweep through the place to see if any books need to be re-shelved. My cleaning lady comes tomorrow morning, so there's no need to vacuum. When we're done, we can go upstairs and order something from takeout. My treat today — and don't you argue with me!"

Dre held up his hands in a defensive gesture. "I'd never dream of it. Let's get started."

* * * *

As Sammy had predicted, it didn't take long for them to get the shop straightened out. As soon as they entered Sammy's kitchen, he handed Dre a stack of menus from delivery places in Beaconville.

"Have you got a hankering for anything?" Dre looked at Sammy. Sammy shook his head.

"No, I'm good with anything. The Chinese is decent, and the pizza place makes a delicious panna cotta."

Dre shifted through the stack until he found the two menus in question. He wasn't a great fan of Chinese food, but he did love a greasy pizza. "How about we order two pizzas, extra-large—one meat lover and one with four cheeses—plus two helpings of panna cotta and one salad."

Sammy grinned. "Low on the greens, I like that. We can take it all to the couch and watch a movie."

"How about *A Fish Called Wanda*?" Dre tried his hardest to look suggestively.

"Great idea. Though I do have to warn you... I'm not sure if you can match up to John Cleese."

"Uh, I bet I do. Wanna know why? Because I, *mo grah thu*, happen to speak fluent demon, which is a lot more erotic than Italian."

"Is it?" Sammy raised a brow. "I haven't heard you speak demon, but I always imagined it would sound a bit like Klingon."

Dre pressed one hand to his chest and the back of the other against his forehead, feigning consternation. "Klingon! I'm wounded. Deeply wounded. The demon tongue is pure poetry." He sighed. "I better start teaching you, so you can appreciate it in its full glory."

Sammy laughed out loud. "You do that." He wrinkled his nose. "After I have a shower. I reek."

"Only of the best things—coffee, muffins and books."

"You charmer. I don't believe you, since you're biased. Can you order our meal? I'm in their database."

Dre saluted. "Will do that. Take your time under the shower."

Sammy sauntered over and pressed a kiss to Dre's lips. "Thank you, Dre." The look in Sammy's eyes told Dre he was thanking him for more than just ordering their dinner. He caressed Sammy's hair, wondering how he had managed to fall so hard for the man in such a short time.

"It's fine, *mo grah thu*. Go shower. We can talk later."

With one last kiss, Sammy vanished through the kitchen door. Once Dre heard the water in the shower running, he took out his cell to make their order. While he waited for Sammy to finish his shower, Dre made himself comfortable in the living room, where Sammy had one of those couches with a seating surface so big that it was impossible not to put your feet up if you wanted to lean against the backrest. The cover was made of a sturdy canvas material in different shades of orange to red with six fluffy pillows in yellow. The floor was done with light hardwood planks, which went well with the white walls and furniture that provided a nice contrast to the colorful couch. A slim wardrobe with the door missing and stocked with books and an entertainment center with gleaming silver surfaces made for an interesting mix.

Dre studied the pictures Sammy had hung on the walls. Most of them were family pictures, showing Sammy from being a baby up to a clumsy teenager who seemed to be made purely of legs and arms, always together with a woman with blonde hair, blue eyes and lightly tanned skin as well as a lean black man with soft, dark eyes. The love in those pictures was palpable. Sammy hadn't told Dre much about his parents. The topic seemed to be too painful for him, and if the pictures were anything to go by, Dre could understand.

The doorbell ended Dre's musings. Since Sammy hadn't come out of the bathroom yet, Dre made his way down to the back door that doubled as the entrance for the apartment. Getting out his wallet with a grin, Dre opened the door. It seemed as if Sammy would have to wait until he could pay for one of their dates, which was just fine with Dre. He liked providing for Sammy.

The delivery guy was still in his teens, with some acne spots on his cheeks, a few patches of brownish stubble growing around his chin and mouth and decidedly too much cheap cologne that did a poor job of masking the stench of puberty sweat. The boy held out the bill but avoided making eye contact.

"That's twenty-five seventy, sir."

Dre felt a strange niggling at the back of his mind, telling him he had heard that voice before. He ignored it, getting out the cash to pay for their dinner. When he handed the boy the money, he looked up from under his baseball cap and his eyes widened, almost as if he were a cartoon character. His mouth opened and closed a few times, doing an impressive impersonation of a fish before he squeaked: "Thank you, sir."

Dre frowned. He *had* heard that voice before, not even a week ago. "You! You're the black terrycloth guy!"

The boy dropped the insulated box, turned on his heels and tried to make a run for it but Dre was faster. He grabbed him by the shoulders and spun him around so fast that the boy practically crashed against his chest.

"Oh no, my friend. You're not going anywhere."

Dre put his wallet back into his jeans pocket, threw the struggling boy over his shoulder, bent down to retrieve the food and went back upstairs. Sammy was out of the shower now, his hair still a bit wet—a look that worked well for him—and was busy carrying cutlery and glasses into the living room. He threw Dre a questioning glance.

"Did you change your mind about the pizza?"

The boy struggled more fiercely on his shoulder when he heard that question, so Dre hurried to put the box with the food down before he placed the boy on his feet, never letting go of him.

"I might still do that. This is one of the little shits who tried to sacrifice you. I thought it would be nice to get some answers."

Sammy gasped at this revelation and started approaching Dre and his prisoner carefully.

"Are you sure?"

"Oh yes." Dre knew his eyes were deep red by now because he was so angry about what Sammy had had to endure. If it hadn't been thanks to the kidnapping that Dre had met Sammy, the boy would already be on a trip through the demon cells in the royal prison to teach him a lesson.

"I'm sorry! I'm really sorry! I never thought you'd appear anyway, and I just wanted Josh and Chase to shut their stupid mouths. I'm sorry. So sorry."

The boy started wailing and Dre felt almost sorry for him. Almost. He bared his fangs at him, which elicited a shriek and more sobbing.

"You summoned a demon and tried to sacrifice a human being because you wanted your friends to shut their mouths? What did they say to you that was so offensive?"

The boy cowered on the floor, his arms over his head to protect himself. "P-p-please! Don't kill me!"

Dre opened his mouth to tell the little shit exactly what he thought of him, but Sammy beat him to it. He approached the weeping boy carefully, put his hand on his shoulder while making soothing sounds in the back of his throat.

"Hey, man, it's fine. It may not seem like it, but Dre and I just want to talk to you. I assume you've already realized how dangerous it was to play with the occult?"

The boy looked up. He had tears and snot staining his face, and his cheeks had taken on an unnaturally deep red color. "Yes. I never thought it would work. I just wanted them to leave me alone."

"Okay, uhm, what's your name?"

"I'm Milo. Milo Tenniel."

"Milo. I'm Sammy. Now, why did you want Chase, I think you said his name was, to leave you alone? Aren't they your friends?"

Milo slowly calmed and Sammy urged him to stand. He still threw wary gazes in Dre's direction but was mainly concentrated on Sammy, who kept on stroking his left shoulder and arm. When he answered, his voice sounded meek, dejected.

"They're not my friends, just kids I know from school."

"And they were teasing you?" Sammy was so calm and understanding. Even though Dre still wanted to teach the boy a lesson, he admired how Sammy got him to talk without using force, though Dre's presence also seemed to encourage cooperation from the boy.

"Yes. They're mean all the time because I'm at school on a scholarship and my mom is a single mother who works double shifts as a waitress. They say I have no place at a fancy private school. Two weeks ago, they cornered me on my way home and threatened to give me a beating. I'd just read a book about demons, so I told them I'd summon one who would hurt them instead." Milo hung his head. "One thing led to another and before I knew it, I had agreed to summon a demon to show them. When the first attempts failed, they got impatient and said they would make me pay. I was glad when you showed up" — he looked at Dre — "because it meant they would finally leave me alone. The sacrifice was Chase's idea. He said he wanted a lot of things, so we needed to give you an incentive, and he thought taking you" — he shifted his attention back to Sammy — "would be easiest, since you live alone." Milo glanced at Dre again.

"I'm so sorry. It was never meant to get that far."

Dre shared a long look with Sammy. If he'd gotten a dollar for every time he'd heard those words — '*It was never meant to get that far*' — in regard to the paranormal world, he still wouldn't have as much money as he had now, but it would come close. Regret about stupid decisions that cost lives seemed to be a very human trait, and ignorance of the paranormal world only carried so far as an apology. Sammy handed him a tissue from a box situated on the dresser. Milo cleaned his nose loudly.

"You must be smart to get a scholarship." Sammy smiled at Milo. The boy shrugged.

"I'm good at math and physics. I want to go to MIT. That's why I'm working at the delivery service. Half the money I give my mom and the other half goes into my college fund."

"Wow, that's impressive! Are you trying for a scholarship to MIT as well?" Dre hadn't planned on being friendly to Milo, but the way the boy talked about his future plans had woken his curiosity. About ten years ago, Barion had thought about studying at MIT, though for some reason or another, he had always postponed it, as was typical for him. Dre admired Milo's focus.

"Yes. A scholarship would be ideal, but the competition is a lot harder than it was for my current school, and I have to be prepared if I only get a partial scholarship—or none at all."

"I guess you need all the money you can get." Sammy looked thoughtful. "Would you be interested in working for me? Now that I'm dating"—a happy smile flitted across his face, as if he couldn't believe it himself—"I could use a part-timer who looks after the shop when I'm not here. And since you know demons are real, you won't be shocked by my more—let's call them interesting—customers. What do you think?"

Milo stared at Sammy with his mouth open. "You're offering me a job after I tried to kill you?"

Dre could understand Milo's amazement. He felt it himself. Sammy grinned like a maniac.

"Well, you said you were sorry, which I believe. You need help, which I can offer. Besides"—Sammy winked — "who says working for me is something you should be grateful for?"

"I don't care how bad it is. I promise that you won't regret it!" Milo had transformed from a crying, miserable mess to an eager puppy. He hesitated a moment before he threw himself into Sammy's arms. "Thank you, thank you, thank you!"

Over Milo's shoulder, Sammy winked at Dre, who cleared his throat. "Fine. You learned your lesson. Now be a good boy and let me have some quality time with my boyfriend."

Milo blushed and stepped away from Sammy. "Of course."

"Come to my shop tomorrow after school, Milo. I can show you around."

"Will do. Thank you, Sammy. Dresalantion." The last was said with a hint of fear. Dre decided to let the boy off the hook, since it seemed as if he would be seeing him more often in the future.

"You can call me Dre. Let me give you your money. I'm sure you still have some delivering to do."

Milo nodded. He took the money and put the two cartons with their pizzas on the small table in front of the couch. "I'm sorry. It's probably cold by now."

"Don't worry. I have that covered." Dre put his hand on Milo's shoulder while leading him to the door. "There we are. Take care."

"Yeah. You too," Milo murmured before he made his way out of the alleyway. Dre watched him go, not sure what to think about this new development. He decided to let it rest for the moment and see if Milo showed up the next day. Basically he welcomed the idea of Sammy having more time for him, so perhaps it wasn't such a bad idea letting the boy work for Sammy. That way, Dre could keep an eye on him.

He made his way back up to the living room, where Sammy was busy slicing the pizzas.

"I'm afraid Milo was right. They're lukewarm at best."

Dre sauntered over to Sammy, to press a kiss on his forehead. "As I already said, I've got this."

He slung his left arm around Sammy's waist, while holding his right hand over the pizza slices. Heat left his body in waves, and in less than a minute, the pizza was steaming again. With a smug grin, Dre turned his head to Sammy. "Told you."

Sammy stared at the pizza with big eyes. "With you around, I can totally sell my microwave. You're way cooler anyway."

The twitching of Sammy's mouth told Dre he was making fun of him. "Wonderful. I've graduated from heating blanket to microwave. I wonder when I'll be something awesome?"

Sammy pretended to think about this for a moment. "You mean like game console level? I don't know. Depends on what other hidden talents you have. Besides, microwaves are valuable kitchen appliances. Did you know that the American engineer Percy Spencer invented the microwave after World War II? The first countertop microwave was sold in 1967, and since then, they've become a standard appliance in home kitchens."

"Fascinating, *mo grah thu*. I bow to your knowledge about something as important as a box for reheating food." Dre chuckled.

"Hey." Sammy slapped him lightly on the arm. "The technology behind it is quite complicated."

"Yes, *mo grah thu*. Now let's eat. I'm starving."

Still grumbling, Sammy let Dre pull him down on the couch. He took the remote control, searched for *A Fish Called Wanda* in his media archive and let it play in the background. They ate their meal in companionable silence. Dre was glad Sammy left him most of the meat lovers pizza and more than half of the four cheeses. To show his gratitude, he only ate half of his panna cotta, leaving the rest to Sammy. After they had eaten, they snuggled on the couch, watching as John Cleese convinced Jamie Lee Curtis to be his. When the credits started to roll, Dre nuzzled Sammy's neck.

"Do you want to talk about what happened today?"

Sammy kissed Dre on the lips. "No. Tomorrow. Tonight, I want to do some exploring. Not all the way, mind you, but I want to get...uhm, acquainted with your body. Is that okay?"

Dre couldn't stand the insecurity in Sammy's voice. His lover should never feel hesitant about voicing his needs. "I would love to do that, *mo grah thu*."

The beautiful smile on Sammy's face almost blinded Dre. "Then let's go." Sammy rose from the couch, taking the cartons and cutlery from their meal with him. On their way to Sammy's bedroom, they put them on the kitchen counter. Dre followed Sammy's lead, ogling his perfect butt, which moved smoothly under the jeans. He couldn't wait to see his man naked for the first time. For all the kissing and groping they had already done, neither had yet taken off their clothes in the company of the other.

Chapter Eight

Sammy's heart hammered against his ribs. For the first time in his life, he was taking another person, a man, to his bedroom. And not just any man... A demon, who happened to be his potential true mate. Sammy wondered briefly how his life could have changed so dramatically in the course of less than a week. It was great, though. And for the first time since his parents had died, Sammy felt the sadness lifting that had permeated his entire being. Dre was like a ray of sunshine in his overcast life, and if he didn't stop with the strange weather metaphors, he would probably start crying.

Sammy stopped in front of his bedroom door. Dre's presence behind him was sure and warm and strong. With trembling fingers, Sammy opened the door and switched on the light before he stepped through. Dre whistled softly behind him.

"Beautiful."

Sammy smiled. "Thank you." The bedroom was the place he was proudest of, right after the shop. The heart of the space was doubtless the bed. Slightly bigger than a king size, the headrest was two foot six inches high, made from black steel that formed an elaborate flower pattern that ran along the sides of the bed to the foot. There, the steel 'grew' into two bedposts that looked like trees, whose branches shadowed half of the bed. Sammy had draped a silken cloth in a light green color over them, creating the feeling as if the bed were indeed under a canopy. Sammy flicked the light switches next to the door, shutting off the main light and activating the dozens of tiny pin lights attached to the steel branches. Every time Sammy saw his beautiful bed, he thanked the genius artist who had designed it.

"It feels as if we're standing in a clearing, complete with fireflies and everything." Dre sounded reverent.

"Exactly the mood I was going for." Sammy looked at the dark green, thick carpet, the walls that were painted in various shades of green flowing into each other and the two dressers made from solid oak. The bedsheet was white, the duvet cover a light orange that always reminded Sammy of the setting sun. "It's my sanctuary."

Dre pulled Sammy close. Without Sammy saying it out loud, Dre seemed to understand what he wanted to tell him — that he was the first person Sammy had ever brought there.

"I'm honored, *mo grah thu.*"

Dre turned him around in his arms and they started kissing. It still felt strange, kissing somebody as beautiful as Dre. Sammy thought he would never tire of the little electric tingle between them whenever their tongues met. And the heat... Dre was always warm, making Sammy feel everything from sheltered to cozy to passionate, depending on the mood. Their kiss deepened and went from playful to scorching within heartbeats. Sammy clung to Dre's strong body, trying to get as close to him as possible until he felt Dre's hands sliding under his T-shirt. Without hesitation, Sammy leaned back a bit, moving his arms over his head to help Dre with getting the fabric off him. Not wanting to be the only one naked, Sammy started tugging at Dre's shirt, though there was no chance he could pull it over his head. Dre was simply too tall. Grinning, Dre grabbed the collar of the shirt and dragged it off.

Their naked torsos met, skin gliding over skin. Sammy marveled at how soft Dre felt, even though his scales were clearly visible. They were small, like a snake's, and easily overlooked because of the intricate silver patterns on the deep red surface. Sammy started following one of the many swirls that started on Dre's chest and lead him down to where the waistband stopped his exploration. Sammy's hand hovered over the button of Dre's jeans. He looked up to silently ask for permission and gasped when he met Dre's deep red gaze. It seemed as if the demon was very much on board with the idea of getting naked. With a boldness fueled by both lust and curiosity, Sammy opened the button, worked the zipper down and started sliding the denim over Dre's narrow hips. Dre had gone commando and his thick, large cock sprang free the moment the fly gaped apart.

Sammy made a sound in the back of his throat that was equal parts arousal, appreciation and fear. He had read enough gay romance to know the human anus was capable of astounding feats, though when he looked at what Dre had to offer, he wondered if it would be enough. At the same time, he felt his inner muscles clench in anticipation. It was confusing enough for Sammy to hesitate. Dre stroked his shoulders.

"Everything okay?"

He sounded a bit worried and very turned on. Sammy shook his head.

"Yes. No. I mean…you're huge!" He hadn't meant to sound quite so…woozy, but Dre's sheer presence did strange things to his head and ability to think clearly.

Dre chuckled. "That's why we're taking things slow, *mo grah thu*. And thank you, by the way."

Sammy looked up in time to see Dre wink at him. He felt immediately at ease, winking back with a smile tugging at the corners of his lips. Dre helped him get the jeans down to his ankles. He stepped out of them before he got rid of his socks as well. Then Dre looked expectantly at Sammy, who suddenly felt very shy. Dre was such a fine man with muscular thighs and toenails that were pointed like claws. For a brief moment, Sammy wondered why Dre's socks didn't have holes in them, but when Dre started working his zipper down after he had opened the button without Sammy noticing it, he could only gasp and hold on to Dre's lower arms for support. Once his pants were gone as well, Dre lifted him up and placed him on the bed. They lay there, stretched out next to each other, and Sammy didn't know what to do. He was curious about Dre's body, wanted to touch him everywhere, follow the swirls of his tattoos, that maybe, hopefully, would someday show on his skin as well, but he didn't know where to begin. Dre's very erect, very large cock seemed like an obvious place, though Sammy didn't want to appear shallow.

"I'm nervous." Dre's warm voice so close to his ear was like Viagra to Sammy's own erection that had grown so hard that it started to hurt.

"Me too. You're so gorgeous. I want to touch you all over but don't know where to start."

Dre grinned and rolled onto his back. "How about you straddle me, which would give my hands a nice place to rest and my eyes the chance to take you fully in while you can start...exploring." He waggled his eyebrows. Sammy started to laugh, which drained his nervousness. Carefully, because he didn't want to appear more awkward than he already felt, Sammy climbed onto Dre. The heat coming from Dre felt great on the skin of his thighs and under his palms. The cock poking at his lower back had Sammy's imagination plunging to the gutter. *No mindless sex today*, he reminded himself sternly. *You want to explore.* He leaned down to give Dre a deep kiss. It took quite a while, and when Dre finally let Sammy up again, he felt a bit dizzy. Drunk on the kiss, Sammy started caressing the tip of a tattooed swirl that started right under Dre's left ear. He followed the complicated pattern, lost it twice, once around the right nipple, the second time at Dre's ribcage, before he tracked it down to his navel.

"They're beautiful. Do they mean anything?" Sammy felt heat rising in his cheeks. What a stupid question! But Dre chuckled, seemingly not offended in the least.

"Actually, they do. The fact that they're silver means I'm royalty. Ordinary demons have black tattoos and warriors' are bronze. Only my father's are golden, because he's the king. We're born with them, which makes choosing a career a lot easier."

Sammy laughed. "Seems like it. And what kind of career is being royalty? Are you exceptionally good at waving?"

Dre tickled Sammy in retaliation until he was out of breath.

"Mercy! I'm sure you have a lot of grave responsibilities."

"I have. And just for the record, demons and waving don't go well together. When you do it with your claws, it's seen as a threat."

As if to heighten his words, Dre let the claws on his right hand grow out. Very carefully he dragged them across Sammy's chest, making him whimper. Sammy knew he probably should be frightened. Dre's claws were long and sharp enough to slice him open like a ripe melon. But all he felt was lust.

"Is that all? Or are the patterns some secret language? Like Elvish?" He moaned when the needle-sharp tips dug into the flesh below his ribcage, not deep enough to draw blood, but hard enough to make him feel them.

Dre's eyes were a deep, blazing red, and he was looking at Sammy as if he wanted to swallow him whole. "Yes, they are a kind of language, but more like the pictographs of the Aztecs than Elvish." He pointed at his right nipple, around which the pattern looked a bit like a nest of coiling snakes. "This here is my name. Well, not really my name, more like what it represents in the demon tongue." Before Sammy could open his mouth to ask, Dre talked on. "Chaos and the ability to navigate it. I can't bring order, but I don't have to, since I own the chaos. This" — he pointed at his navel — "represents my family, which has ruled over the demon world since the beginning of time."

Sammy listened, completely fascinated. "So the places where it looks as if there's a nest of tattoos are actual words. What about the long lines between? Are they there just to connect the different words?"

Dre smiled, obviously pleased by Sammy's interest. "Yes and no. Some of them are words themselves, others are mere links. The demon tongue is complicated because it uses pictures as well as words to convey meaning. Have you ever seen one of those graffiti paintings where you realized it was actually a word, but you could only read it after somebody told you what it was supposed to mean?"

Sammy nodded. He'd always admired that kind of art.

"It's a bit like that with my tattoos. If you know what they're supposed to mean, it's clear as the day. You'll understand once I've taught you."

Sammy started following another swirl with the tip of his index finger. "Are you sure I'll be able to learn it? It looks awfully complicated."

Dre grabbed his other hand to press a kiss on his palm. "You're a very smart man, *mo grah thu*. You'll figure it out in no time."

Sammy smiled. "Thank you." He shifted a bit on Dre's stomach. The movement had the tip of Dre's cock gliding along his spine. The sudden coldness when the air hit the wet trail Dre's cockhead had left made Sammy shudder.

"Oh God, Dre. I'm not sure I can stick to just exploring. You're so hot."

Dre's answer was a whimpering sound deep in his throat. "Don't tempt me, Sammy. We're supposed to take it slow." He jerked his hips upward, lifting

Sammy's knees off the mattress. A feverish gleam made his eyes appear almost fluorescent. Sammy groaned.

"Do you think jerking each other off counts as taking it slow?"

"It does now!" Dre growled. He tightened his grip on Sammy's hips before he rolled them sideways. Then he pulled Sammy as close to himself as possible, trapping both their hard cocks between their stomachs. Sammy instinctively slung his arm around Dre's body to help him. Dre maneuvered one of his hands between them, engulfing their shafts. If Sammy hadn't been so turned on, he might have felt embarrassed by the difference in size, but at the moment, all he cared about was that his cock was almost completely swallowed by Dre's big hand and that the heat and texture of Dre's cock—slightly raspy where the scales were elevated by the thick veins underneath while wonderfully smooth where the skin spanned the flesh—had him close to exploding.

"So good, Dre. It feels so good."

"Yes, *mo grah thu*. You're perfect." Dre panted heavily in Sammy's ear, while he started stroking their shafts. Sammy followed the movement with his hips, chasing the friction that soon would have him exploding against Dre's chest.

"Close, Dre. So close. Need you... Harder."

"Sammy!"

The moment Dre's hand closed like a vise around their cocks, Sammy felt the pulsing start in his balls, race along his shaft, then his seed shot out at the same time Dre coated his stomach with his release. The warm stickiness from their combined essence felt so good on Sammy's skin that his cock twitched with interest, even though he felt like he just spent everything he had. The touch of Dre's hand on his cock was both soothing and painful, making his nerve endings scream from overstimulation. Dre murmured in a language Sammy assumed was his mother tongue, because all he could make out in the musical lilt was his own name. He shifted a bit, to re-establish skin contact in the places where they had parted during their orgasms and a sharp pain in his back told him Dre's claws must have come out. The realization that being with him had made Dre lose his composure quickly morphed the pain into a warm tingling of pleasure. All of a sudden, the pressure in his back vanished.

"Sorry." Dre winced. "I didn't mean to hurt you."

"Shh, it's fine. It feels good to be able to make you go crazy."

"Always, *mo grah thu*. Always."

They started kissing while the cum dried on their bodies. Sammy found he didn't care one bit. After they had both come down from their high and their skin had started to itch, they went into the bathroom to have a shower. It felt natural to do that together with Dre, even though it was a challenge to fit them both into the shower stall. Sammy had always meant to get a new, huge shower, but had postponed the project until now. As it seemed, a bigger one had just become a necessity. When they were both clean, they changed the sheets on the bed, fetched a bottle of water from the kitchen then snuggled under the covers.

"This was nice. I like being with you, Dre. A lot."

"I like being with you, too. We should do this more often, to make sure it's always that great."

Sammy yawned and chuckled at the same time, which led to a coughing fit. When he was able to talk again, he said: "Yeah. I'd be disappointed if this were a one-time thing."

"You're tired, *mo grah thu*."

Sammy yawned even louder. "Yes. 'Twas a long day."

Dre kissed Sammy on the forehead before he pressed him flush against his strong body. "Sleep, *mo grah thu*. We can talk later."

* * * *

Sammy was jostled awake by the sound of his alarm going off. It took him a moment to realize that the warm presence behind him wasn't a hot water bottle but Dre, who had kept him nice and cozy throughout the night. Blindly, he fumbled for the button to shut the blaring sound off. Why on earth had he chosen such an ear-piercing ring to wake up in the morning? Oh, yeah, he slept through anything else. He finally found the right button and hit it with more force than was strictly necessary. When he tried to cuddle back into Dre's warm embrace, he found his demon lover crouching on the bed, claws out, eyes a deep red, lips pulled back to show his impressive fangs and at least two feet taller than he had been when they'd gone to sleep. Sammy suddenly realized that he hadn't seen Dre in his demon form yet, though being confronted with it first thing in the morning wasn't how he had wanted to start his day.

"*What* was that?"

Even Dre's voice had changed to a deeper cadence close to a growl, which sent shivers down Sammy's spine and had his morning wood twitching in interest.

"Uhm, my alarm. You see...getting up in the morning is hard for me —"

"So you'd rather let yourself go deaf? I mean, I've heard my fair share of battle cries, but this? I have no words."

The fangs started receding. Before Sammy knew what he was doing, he leaned forward to touch them. Dre made a strangled noise, a bit like a kitten mewling for its mother. Sammy was fascinated. Dre's canines were almost as long as his hand, the tips pointed like needles and razor-sharp as he found out when the skin of his right index finger was sliced open. A thin smear of blood coating the fang gave Sammy a shiver. He wanted to withdraw his hand, but Dre grabbed his wrist. His eyes were still a deep red, though darker now and filled with lust.

"Let me kiss it better."

Sammy watched Dre's tongue snaking out to lick over the small tear in his skin. Again, he knew he should be afraid. Again, all he felt was arousal and a bone-deep knowledge that he was safe.

"Is this the real you?" With his free hand, Sammy indicated Dre's huge body. Dre finished licking the blood before he leaned back a bit with an amused glint in his eyes.

"I'm always my real self."

"Don't you start quoting Esme Weatherwax on me. You know what I mean."

Dre chuckled. "I do. You have to admit, though that this was too good an opportunity to pass up."

Sammy just furrowed his forehead.

"Fine. No, I'm just partially shifted. I have wings and my hair turns into scales. But this is as big as I get."

"Which is impressive." Sammy let his eyes wander over Dre's gorgeous body. He was even more muscular in his shifted form and farther down... Sammy gulped and hurried to look back into Dre's eyes. He wasn't ready for what appeared to be a third leg between the demon's thighs. Dre smirked. Gradually, he shrank back to the huge form Sammy was used to. "Better?"

"I honestly don't know. You're beautiful in both forms. I just didn't expect you to go all demon on me first thing in the morning."

"Sorry about that. I thought we were being attacked. Is this how you wake up every morning?"

Sammy shrugged. "I'm a sound sleeper."

"Mm-m, and a cuddler, not that I mind."

The suggestive gleam in Dre's eyes had Sammy's thoughts going in a direction that would do neither of them any good at the moment. Breakfast. They needed breakfast.

"Are you hungry? I think I have the ingredients for scrambled eggs with toast in the fridge."

Dre reached for Sammy's waist to pull him flush against his deliciously warm, firm body. "Sounds great. If you don't want to cook, though, we can always go to Paris. I know this nice little café…"

Sammy slung his arms around Dre as far as they would go and pressed a kiss between his pecs. "That's so sweet of you. But I think I want to make breakfast for you. Show off my cooking skills — the few I have."

"In case you haven't noticed, I've already fallen for you. There's no need to impress me anymore."

The words were spoken in a light tone, but they reminded Sammy of all the baggage that had been dumped in his lap the day before. Dre must have picked up on his change of mood, because he crushed Sammy even tighter to his body.

"Let's go have breakfast and talk. Okay? Or would you rather have me leave, give you some space?"

Dre was so considerate that it almost made Sammy cry. "No. We're in this together. What good would me freaking out over it on my own do? Come on. Let's get going."

Sammy used the bathroom first and started working on the eggs and toast while Dre took his turn. Once he had their breakfast scooped onto two plates, they sat down with two glasses of milk, only to stare at their food without eating it. Finally, Dre cleared his throat.

"Let's try to eat before we talk. It would be a shame to let the food go to waste."

Sammy nodded in agreement. He started shoveling the eggs into his mouth, not really tasting anything. His heart was heavy, and his stomach felt as if he were swallowing lead weights instead of pieces of buttered toast while his thoughts swirled through his head like a flock of disoriented doves. When he had eaten half of his plateful, he put the fork and knife down and simply started talking, letting it all flow out of his mouth without bothering to make it sound plausible, since he figured he'd never be able to do that.

"I like you, Dre. No, I'm sure I love you. I know that we've only been on four dates so far and it's *very* early, but the things I feel for you and when you're around, even when you're not around— What I'm trying to say is, if this isn't love, then I don't know what is. To think I might be your mate is both wonderful and terrifying. Last night was—wow, just wow. I feel so in tune with you, I'm not afraid, I just sense being with you is the safest place I can be. And I'm terrified of what will happen to all that once we... Once we find out I'm not it, not your mate. And what if I am? There are just so many 'what ifs' and you're the first good thing happening to me love-wise since my parents died. I can't lose you, but I also can't imagine living in limbo for a prolonged time. I want to know, and I don't want to know. Gosh, I don't make any sense at all."

Sammy buried his face in his hands. When he felt Dre's hand on his shoulder, he slowly looked up. The passion he saw in Dre's eyes had tears streaming down Sammy's cheeks.

"It's fine, *mo grah thu*. You make perfect sense. It's essentially what I feel, as well. I've been waiting for my mate for so long. The thought of you being it makes my heart beat faster in anticipation, yet, at the same time, I fear what will be if you aren't. We're so good together and I don't want to wait even a second longer. I wish we could just stay like this forever and never have to find out."

They looked at each other, each lost in the gaze of the other. Sammy found himself in the depths of Dre's soul, felt a piece of the demon inside his own. It was as if they were already one, and the thought of it just being the rush of the moment was like a spike right through Sammy's heart. It was Dre who finally broke the silence.

"Let's wait two more weeks, *mo grah thu*. Let's enjoy those weeks as if I were a mortal, just as you are, and as if you didn't know about true mates. Let's be just two guys, getting to know each other, having fun. When those two weeks are up, we face reality."

"A dream. Just for the two of us." Sammy's voice was barely above a whisper. He couldn't manage anything louder. "A dream to remember."

"Yes. Our dream. Our patch of perfection."

They kissed — slowly, sensually, full of love and with all the gentleness they had for each other. Sammy slung his arms around Dre's neck, never wanting to let go, but the need for oxygen grew quite strong after some time and he had to lean back a bit to breathe. Dre smiled at him, still with a hint of sadness, though he was obviously determined to let deeds follow his words.

"When do you have to open the shop?"

Sammy glanced at the watch on the stove. "Now." He chuckled. Dre pressed a kiss to his nose. "Is it okay if I stay today? Maybe I can help a bit."

"I'd love you to stay, Dre. If it's not too boring for you…"

"Never. I get to watch my favorite human all day. What's boring about that?"

Sammy laughed and swatted Dre's upper arm playfully. "Sweet talker."

"You love it."

"I do."

They put the plates and cutlery in the dishwasher and hastened down to open the shop.

Chapter Nine

"Backpack with two Thermoses of hot tea?"

"Check."

"Two hassocks to keep our butts warm when we have our picnic?"

"Check."

"Warm clothes, not that you need them..." Sammy looked at Dre, who was busy crossing off the items on their list of things they needed for their trip to Sweden. A quick check on the web had told them that the temperatures in Sweden were still chilly, hence the need for proper outdoor gear, at least for Sammy.

"Check."

"Camera to shoot pictures of any interesting wildlife or fauna?"

"Check."

"Paper and crayons to trace the Tanum Petroglyphs?"

Dre grinned broadly and held a leather tube with a strap in the air. "I actually found those cool rectangular crayons, you know, the ones that look like rubbers?"

Sammy frowned. "I always wondered what those are called. What colors?"

"Traditional red, of course."

Sammy smiled happily. He couldn't wait for their adventure to begin. Dre had stayed with him the entire week and Sammy had loved it — so much, in fact, that he was beginning to think it didn't matter if he really wasn't Dre's mate. If only he could have a few years like the last week with his gorgeous demon, Sammy was willing to face the heartache when he and Dre had to part ways — or so he told himself. Deep down he knew that his wishful thinking was turning their two-week dream into a reality that might never come to pass, and every time he looked into Dre's eyes, he knew the demon was doing the same. Sammy wondered if something could become reality when two people only wished for it hard enough.

A kiss on his temple broke him from his bittersweet musings. "Where were you just now, *mo grah thu*?"

Sammy sighed and snuggled into Dre's warm embrace. "Somewhere I probably shouldn't go at the moment. I want to fully enjoy the here and now."

Dre's breath ghosted over the side of Sammy's face like a soft caress. "I know, *mo grah thu*. I feel the same." He straightened. "Let's get going. We have a lot of tracing to do."

"I can't wait." Sammy grabbed the backpack and slung his arms around Dre's waist. By now he was used to traveling demon style, which had him ruined for planes and cars and any other means of moving from point A to B. Why bother when all one needed was a demon to jump places all over the world? They arrived in Tanum, Sweden, in a small clearing in the forest, where nobody was likely to see them. Even if somebody had witnessed them popping out of thin air, Dre's magic saw to it that the person in question simply forgot immediately. Still, in the day and age of cell phone cameras, being careful was paramount.

The air was colder than Sammy had expected and instinctively he turned toward Dre to take advantage of his hot boyfriend, pun fully intended, while he clumsily tried to close the zipper of his jacket. Dre chuckled deeply, the sound almost as warming as the actual heat coming off the demon. As soon as Sammy was bundled up, Dre slung the backpack over his shoulder—it was ridiculous how tiny it looked on him—grabbed Sammy's now-mitten-clad hands and started leading him toward one of the spots where the petroglyphs were. The huge stones were scattered everywhere in the area, and Sammy looked forward to finding the most interesting ones. It was a bit like Easter egg hunting, only with huge rocks.

They had come early enough that not too many people were at the Vitlycke Museum, which gave them a chance to marvel at the Bridal Couple, one of the most famous of the petroglyphs. It was beautiful in its simplicity, a few lines expressing everything there was to say about the joys of bonding with the right person. Even though the carving was rather crude, it spoke to Sammy on a deep level, making him yearn for what he could have with Dre.

"So beautiful. I hope this is going to be us." Dre voiced Sammy's thoughts as if he had taken them directly from his mind. It could have been creepy if Sammy hadn't seen it as proof that he had to be Dre's mate. Why else would they be so perfectly in tune?

"Me too." Sammy looked at Dre with a hint of curiosity. "Do we get a wedding ceremony? Or is it done with the bite?"

"Usually it's done with the bite. It's considered all the ceremony true mates need. But if you want something more formal than scorching hot sex, we can do whatever you wish."

"Spoken like a true husband. I like it." The joke was a bit heavy in Sammy's mouth, but this was their dream. He could pretend they were engaged.

Dre chuckled. "Whatever you wish, *mo grah thu*. I'll give you the world."

"I only need you."

"Stop it or we're going right back to your bedroom, Sammy. You're killing me here."

Sammy turned in Dre's arms and rubbed his cheek on what he could feel of the chiseled abs beneath the thick jacket. Not that Dre needed it, but it helped keep up the magic concealing him. Funnily enough, people had no problem overlooking a seven-foot mountain of a man with red skin and silver tattoos, but their minds drew the line at inappropriate clothing. It was a mystery. When thinking about such things, Sammy often wondered if there was a creator god or goddess somewhere, laughing their ass off at how many jokes they had managed to build into humanity.

"An interesting suggestion. Now the question is are you just horny or do you want to avoid facing me in our little challenge of wisdom?"

Dre snorted. "Hah, as if a puny human could outwit the second son of the demon king!"

"Machu Picchu is all I say."

"Let me respond with Canada."

Sammy leaned back a little so they could look each other in the eyes. "Draw?"

Dre's eyes turned a beautiful shade of crimson. "Too late. Let's settle this here and now."

Sammy lifted his chin with utter determination. "Fine. I'll show you puny."

"It's on, squirt."

They ended their embrace, though Dre kept Sammy's hand in his when they headed for the trail in Aspeberget.

* * * *

"Oh man, that was great! And I totally wiped the floor with your sorry ass!" Dre watched as Sammy did a little victory dance in his kitchen, his eyes sparkling like diamonds, cheeks adorably flushed from the cold.

"You wish. Though that little tidbit about the fertility slides was good—not as good as my knowledge about the battle at Tollense, but nice."

"Hah, Tollense doesn't count, because that's in Germany, not in the Tanum area." Sammy waggled his eyebrows triumphantly.

"I say it does because many of the petroglyphs show scenes of war, and the battle at Tollense happened during the Bronze Age as well. It's referred to as probably the first real war in the history of mankind, which I admit is kind of sad. Still...it counts."

"I say that's cheating." Sammy stuck his tongue out, which Dre took as his cue to approach his man and kiss him senseless. He had found out quickly that this was the easiest way to make Sammy shut up. Plus, it felt incredible.

When they both had to breathe again, Dre looked down into Sammy's beautiful eyes. "What do you think, *mo grah thu*? Shall we shower then have dinner at that lovely French restaurant in Toulouse I told you about or do you want to stay here and order takeout?"

Sammy blinked, which made him look all kinds of adorable. "As much as I'd like to go to Toulouse, I'm just too tired to get dressed again. Let's shower, order in then laze on the couch. Maybe do some exploring of the more carnal nature?"

His grin was probably meant to be seductive, but Sammy apparently was very tired. He looked like a mole who had just broken the surface. Dre laughed out loud and swept Sammy in his arms.

"Yes to all of the above, though I'm not sure about the carnal things. You look beat, *mo grah thu*."

Sammy yawned. "I'll get my second wind once I've eaten. Promise."

"Yes, *mo grah thu*. Whatever you say."

Dre carried Sammy into the shower and, as he had anticipated, into bed when Sammy fell asleep before dessert.

Chapter Ten

"I think I'm going to be sick." Dre watched his reflection in the mirror, wondering if it was possible for demons to throw up. He'd never heard of it, since demons didn't get human diseases, but right now he felt as if his dinner wanted to make a reappearance, which would be a shame, because it had been delicious.

"You're going to be fine. Those are my friends, my family. They're going to love you." Dre was sure Sammy tried to sound reassuring. He would have probably appreciated his efforts more if there hadn't been a slight tremor to his boyfriend's voice. They both were nervous as all hell, ramping each other up. No amount of dessert or heavy petting had been able to calm them down.

Dre splashed some cold water into his face before he straightened his back. Everything in him yearned to turn into his demon form to present a menacing front to the world. But if he wanted Sammy's friends to like him, he had to be approachable — or at least more so than an eight-foot demon with claws sharp enough to perform surgery with them, a wing span that just wasn't made for inside and fangs so long that it became almost impossible to speak once they were fully out.

He had shown his true form to Sammy, who was at first suitably impressed then couldn't get enough of it. After their trip to Sweden, they had spent the rest of the weekend visiting places where Dre could fly with Sammy. To him it was pure heaven that Sammy accepted his demon form so easily, but he knew Sammy's friends wouldn't be so relaxed. From what Sammy had told him, they all were powerful paranormals themselves, and how they managed to have regular book club meetings without killing each other and destroying the book shop in the process remained a mystery to Dre.

After his meeting with Mavis and Maribell, he had done some research on the whole group, and even though he would have probably been able to best them in a fight, he was still glad they had grudgingly accepted him. Those two were a lot more than met the eye, and Dre wouldn't challenge their wrath if he could avoid it. The two alpha werewolves, Declan and Troy, worried him as well. For two alphas to live without a pack and have nobody interfering was unheard of. It spoke a lot of their position within the shifter world that nobody dared to bother them. Emilia, the vampire, was another enigma. Vampires and werewolves mixed about as well as demons and everybody else. Still, she seemed to have no problem meeting regularly with two very powerful shifters. Perhaps it was because she was from the oldest line of vampires, who could trace their ancestors back to Lilith herself. Having such an ancient family at her back gave her a lot of freedom. Amber and Jon, the banshee and the zombie, were the least threatening, though, thanks to Sammy's warning, Dre wouldn't accept any baked goods from Amber.

"You're going to be okay, Dre." Sammy hugged him from behind. *"We're* going to be okay."

Dre put his hands on Sammy's wrists and enjoyed the tingles that radiated through his body from where their skin connected. "I just want them to like me."

"They will. And if not, it's their loss because you're the greatest guy I ever met."

"You're just saying that to get another massage with a happy ending." Dre chuckled.

"Doesn't make it untrue though."

Dre definitely noticed the interest Sammy's cock took in his words, as well as the lack of denial of his statement. During their exploring of each other's bodies Sammy had lost most of his shyness. *The Guide to Successful and Satisfying Sex with a Paranormal* had helped a lot. Dre would have never thought that reading it together could be a source of so much fun and sensual moments. It had been an eye-opener to him. Never before had Dre laughed so much during sex—even if they hadn't gone all the way yet. He was fascinated how easily he and Sammy could change from seriously turned on to laughing so hard that their bellies ached. It made him even more determined to keep Sammy, true mate or not.

"No, it does not. Unfortunately, we don't have time to indulge in happy endings at the moment. We need to go downstairs."

Sammy pouted, but let go of Dre's waist. "Fine, be all logical about it. I just want to point out that Milo is handling the shop pretty well."

That the boy did. Dre had to give him that. It had taken Milo only a week to immerse himself in the workings of the shop. He made a mean café latte and knew the stock almost as well as Sammy himself. The boy seemed to blossom under the calming influence of all the books.

"You're right. But didn't he say something about having to work at the pizza delivery tonight?"

Sammy slapped his forehead. "I forgot. Damn. Let's get downstairs."

On their way out of the apartment, Dre grabbed his copy of the *Chronicles of Corum*, which he had read thoroughly. Since he wasn't likely to sway Sammy's friends with the fact that he was a demon, he wanted to win them over with his love for and knowledge about books.

After they had sent Milo off, Dre watched Sammy operating the coffee maker to create everyone's favorite drink while pacing around nervously. When he heard a door open and close again, he almost jumped out of his skin. Sammy's muffled laughter broke him out of his stupor.

"Easy, Dre. It's just Jon."

Dre looked in the direction Sammy indicated and saw a lean man of middle height standing in front of the section for historic books. His hair was dark black and hung around his face like a veil. He wore black jeans, a blue shirt and fluffy pink slippers. Dre so wanted to look twice but didn't want to appear rude, so he kept his gaze firmly trained on Jon's eyes, which were of a stunning emerald green peeping through the long strands of his hair.

"Hi, Jon, I'm Dre, Sammy's boyfriend."

Jon nodded without extending his hand. Dre already knew the zombie didn't like skin contact, so he wasn't insulted.

"Hi, Dre. Nice to meet you. If you don't mind me asking, on a scale from zero to ten, how dangerous are demons?"

Dre glanced at Sammy in search for help, but the little traitor pretended to be busy with the coffee maker.

"Uhm, if you're going strictly after the power a demon can wield, we're a solid ten, though I do like to point out that violence against anybody in the human realm is very much frowned upon. Our main directive is blending in so we can partake in the wonders the human mind can create."

Dre wasn't sure if he wasn't laying it on a bit too thick. Jon was watching him with wide eyes and even pushed back his hair to get a better look at Dre.

"You're quoting *Star Trek*. I already like you. Are you team Kirk, Picard or Janeway?"

"Tough one. I'm all for an all-cast team with Picard, Spock, Seven of Nine and Chakotay, because I dig the tattoos."

Jon seemed to think about that statement. His shoulders were huddled, as if he wanted to make himself smaller, a clear sign that he was very shy. "I'm with you, though I'd like to add Data. I think he and Spock would make a cute couple."

Before Dre could find an answer to this mind-boggling idea, the chimes above the shop door announced more visitors. The first ones to enter were Mavis and Maribell, closely followed by two extremely handsome men who could only be the wolf shifters. There was just something about those who shared their body with an animal spirit that always made them stand out. The blond guy was about to close the door then opened it wide again, stepping slightly to the side to let two females in. The smaller one had short, green hair and wore enough jewelry to open a store, thus had to be the banshee. The second one was almost as tall as the two wolf shifters, with long, chestnut-colored hair and the perfect pearly complexion that only vampires possessed. When she greeted him, her voice had that soft cadence no human could resist. Thankfully, Dre was mostly immune to the powers of other paranormals.

"Hello, handsome, you must be Dre, Sammy's boyfriend. Mavis and Maribell have told us everything about you." Emilia looked him up and down, her expression unreadable.

Somehow Dre knew it was nothing good. He also tried to ignore the thinly veiled threat she had delivered. These people were only trying to look out for Sammy, a fact Dre reminded himself of constantly.

"He likes Picard and Chakotay."

The statement came out of nowhere, and when Dre looked back at Jon, the zombie seemed to shrink in on himself.

"Picard and Chakotay? You're kidding me, right? Kirk and Spock are the kings." The banshee, Amber, Dre remembered, looked at him with a frown. He opened his mouth to respond, but either Declan or Troy, Dre wasn't sure which one, beat him to it.

"Amber, please, do we have to go over this again? Nobody says it wasn't a heroic deed by William Shatner to suck his belly in for I don't know how many episodes, but he still holds no candle to Seven of Nine. No sucking in of body parts there." The wolf winked at Dre before he hastily jumped backward when Amber poked him with her index finger between the ribs.

"Do you even listen to yourself? How sexist can you get?"

"Is that a trick question? You do know we're werewolves, don't you?" It was the other wolf who spoke. Emilia rolled her eyes.

"Please, we've been over this. Stop using your genetic makeup as an excuse. You're smart enough to be better than that."

"You're taking all the fun out of this." The wolf who had first spoken actually pouted. "I still stand by my words. Seven of Nine is the best."

"What all of you seem to forget is the beauty that lies within maturity." Maribell sounded soothing. "Which is why Chakotay and Picard are the kings."

"Data and Spock." Jon's voice was firm, if a bit hushed, as if he wasn't sure if he wanted to be heard.

"Guys, can we please stop with the *Star Trek* discussion or do I have to remind you of the great *Avengers* incident last summer?" Sammy carried a tray full of different beverages to the two tables in front of the counter. After some mumbled sentences that Dre was glad he couldn't hear clearly, they all sat down on the couches. He made sure to be next to Sammy, casually putting an arm around his shoulders. With two virile werewolves in close proximity, he felt the need to stake his claim. Sammy didn't seem to mind, so everything was fine.

"Everybody, this is Dre, my boyfriend. Dre, you've already met Mavis and Maribell…and Jon. These are Amber, Emilia, Declan and Troy." The introduction wasn't really needed, since Dre had—with the exception of the werewolves—already figured out who was who, but he appreciated the formality. It made everything appear more civilized, which was important when so many different paranormals met.

Dre nodded at each person. "It's a pleasure meeting you all. Thank you for having me."

Declan grinned broadly. "I have a feeling you'd be here anyway. Nice meeting you. Please don't go all demon on us." The words sounded nonchalant, though Dre could feel the underlying tension. He decided to play with open cards.

"Okay, here's the deal. Whatever you've heard about demons is probably true. Whatever experiences you've had with demons, I sincerely apologize for the behavior of my kind. And let me assure you that I'm not here to blow a fuse then go on a rampage. I'm genuinely interested in Sammy, which should be no surprise to you, since you all surely know what a kind, caring and wonderful person he is. As his friends, I want to impress you somewhat badly, because if things work out the way I intend them to, we're going to see a lot of each other." He looked around, maintained eye contact with everyone in the group. For a moment, there was silence, until Mavis clapped her hands.

"Well said, Dre. You get your chance — and not just because you provide some additional eye candy for my sweetheart and me." Maribell leaned over to give her wife a kiss on the cheek.

"What? Are we no longer good enough for you?" Troy threw his arms in the air.

"Whatever makes you think we weren't talking about you two?" Mavis winked at the two wolves. Declan pressed his hands to his heart as if he were mortally wounded.

"Where's the love, Mavis?"

"Probably died a heroic death, just like Corum." Sammy grinned. "Notice my subtle attempt at changing the topic?"

"I thought we were having fun!" Amber grabbed a blueberry muffin from the tray on the Smaug and Drogon table and sniffed it with a dreamy smile. Sammy rolled his eyes.

"You were arguing about *Star Trek* and making my boyfriend uncomfortable. How is that fun?"

"As if you've never argued about geek trivia. That *Avengers* incident was because of your insistence that the Scarlet Witch could have wiped the floor with Thanos." Amber crossed her arms, causing the countless amulets to jingle.

A hard glint entered Sammy's eyes. "I stand by that. If Mantis with her glowing feelers was able to enter Thanos' mind, the Scarlet Witch should have had a field day with him."

"He's right about that one, Amber. I think all the Avengers and their powers were downplayed in that film." Troy snatched a chocolate chip muffin off the tray and polished it off with two bites.

"I still hate that so many of them had to die. That's just not how a superhero movie is supposed to end." Jon looked at his lap while speaking.

"Which brings us back to our initial topic." Mavis smiled softly. "Heroes die all the time. We've seen that with Corum, Hercules, Beowulf, Siegfried and many others. Perhaps it would be interesting to look up at which point exactly mankind stopped killing their heroes and gave them sequels instead."

The others nodded. Dre thought about it for a moment. "You're kind of right, Mavis. Though I do want to point out that the old heroes, like Hercules or Siegfried, have their sequels as well. They're just packed into one huge tale. Or, in the case of Ulysses, two tales. We see them growing up and eventually dying in battle or by treason. I don't think that's too different from how humans treat modern heroes. They just have better CGI now."

"Well said, man!" Declan chuckled. "The question is, why do we expect our heroes to be a certain way? Is this something ingrained in the human psyche? Troy and I have found an article about how the need to paint things in black and white played a huge role when heroes were invented."

"I imagine things were definitely easier back then in terms of what your mind had to process. The world was a significantly smaller place, where often the village over the next hill seemed outlandish. I can see how people wanted their heroes to be clear-cut. Modern technology has robbed people of that narrow-mindedness, which is probably the reason why so many wish it to come back. It can be scary out there." Sammy snuggled closer to Dre while saying this, and Dre pressed a kiss on his forehead.

"I agree, *mo grah thu*. My father always says life was less complicated when he was young. More violent as well, though, which is the reason he's glad those times are over. The way humans portray their heroes reflects how they're coping with reality. I have to admit that I wasn't overly impressed by *Infinity War*, but I had a feeling it was some kind of allegory. Humanity is now at a point where heroes are no longer enough to save the people. They have to be active themselves and that frightens them."

"You're right, Dre, though I think it's not just humans who have to take on a more active role. Change is never easy, and the way some people, namely my father, cling to the old just because it's familiar is sad and infuriating at the same time." Emilia took a sip from her coffee.

"Preserving the old is not always a bad thing, dear, provided it's only the good parts." Maribell smiled at Mavis. "Without all those wonderful old spells, my wife and I would just be two helpless grandmas at the mercy of society."

Amber snorted. "As if. Nothing about you two is helpless. And I always thought witch magic doesn't need any spells?"

"It doesn't. They just make it easier to focus. And I always liked babbling mysteriously in a foreign language. It's all about setting the right mood." Mavis winked and they all started to laugh. Dre found he liked Sammy's friends a lot. After their initial wariness, they seemed to be accepting him just fine now, a show of trust he was determined not to disappoint.

The discussion kept meandering around the general concept of the hero and the reasons for the changes for another hour until Amber announced she had to go because of another appointment. At this hour, it was probably one tied to her being a banshee, so nobody asked any questions. Since it was already past ten, the others left with her, after they had decided what book to read next. Since *The Chronicles of Corum* had sent them in the direction of strange creatures, they agreed to read H. P. Lovecraft's *Cthulu Cycle,* along with *The Witcher of Salem* by Wolfgang Hohlbein. Dre found the idea great, because he knew H. P. Lovecraft had been friends with a demon and gotten many of his ideas for the *Cthulu Cycle* from her, though he would wait with divulging that piece of information until their next meeting. No need to spoil the fun.

After Jon was back in his cellar and the others out of the door, Dre lifted Sammy into his arms and carried him upstairs. It was time for bed.

Chapter Eleven

"I think I'm going to be sick." Sammy saw Dre raising his brows at his declaration.

"I think you're stealing my line here." His huge demon boyfriend leaned over the table to press a kiss on Sammy's forehead. It was Friday, the middle of their two-week dream, and Dre had finally declared Sammy to be ready to meet Barion, Dre's younger brother. With the time for their visit drawing closer, Sammy got more and more nervous, while his respect for Dre grew exponentially. He was a wreck from the prospect of just meeting one member of Dre's family. How Dre had managed to face all of Sammy's friends at once without biting his claws down to little stumps remained a mystery to Sammy.

"*Mo grah thu*, see it like this. You're going to be in a mansion dating back to 1163 in the very area where Vlad Dracul lived and fought the Turks." Dre pulled Sammy into his lap, lowering his voice to a conspiratorial whisper. "And I happen to know that

Barion has this huge library with hundreds of old books, even though I doubt he has read many of them."

Sammy's eyes lit up at these words. "Hundreds you say?" He bit his lip. "But isn't it terribly impolite to visit him for his books?"

"*Mo grah thu*, you're a delight." Dre kissed him deeply, which gave Sammy all kinds of ideas, none of which were feasible since they would be leaving — now, as a quick glance toward the clock told him.

"I think we have to go now, Dre." Sammy swallowed hard.

Dre got up, not bothering to let go of Sammy, which Sammy appreciated greatly. He loved being held by Dre, his strength and warmth giving Sammy a feeling of belonging that he hadn't felt since he'd lost his parents. His demon boyfriend sliced time and space with one of his lethal claws, and before Sammy could blink twice, they were standing in a stone hall with an impressive vaulted ceiling and a floor obviously made from antique wood. Still snuggled in Dre's arms, Sammy looked around with huge eyes, drinking in the wonder of the mansion he was now in.

A polite cough behind Dre had them both turning around. Sammy knew immediately he was looking at a sibling of Dre's. Apart from the fact that they were supposed to visit his brother, the family resemblance was striking. Barion was blue where Dre was red, but his tattoos were of the same silver hue, he was as tall as Dre and he had similar facial features.

"Hello, Barion. May I introduce you to Sammy?" Dre put Sammy on his feet while his brother approached them with a broad smile, showing all his gleaming teeth.

"Hello, Sammy. It's so good to meet you. I've never seen Dre so happy. I'm so glad you're putting up with him." Barion grabbed Sammy's hand and shook it violently.

"Hello, Barion. Nice to meet you too. And I'm not sure who is putting up with who. Dre is simply perfect."

"Aww, young love. You two are so sweet. Come on. Dinner is ready." Barion hadn't let go of Sammy's hand and was now dragging him toward a doorway to the left.

"You cooked?" Dre didn't sound impressed, rather frightened if Sammy thought about it.

"Don't worry, big bro, I didn't do it myself. I learned my lesson, though I do want to emphasize that it wasn't solely my fault. There was something wrong with the recipe."

"Barion, we had to burn down the kitchen!"

"How was I supposed to know that sugar could explode?" Barion sounded defensive, while Dre just rolled his eyes.

"I have a friend you simply have to meet. Just promise me not to enter a kitchen with her." Sammy smiled. He loved the playful banter between the brothers.

"So where did you get the food?" They had reached a dining room with a huge round wooden table and heavy wooden chairs with thick, lime-green upholstery. While Sammy was busy staring at the stag skull that was plastered with what appeared to be emeralds and rubies, Dre turned to his brother.

"I can't tell you my sources, big bro. You should know that."

"Barion, who made the food? I'm not going to let Sammy eat something when I don't know where you got it."

Barion made a face. "Fine, Mr. Overbearing. I went to Zenobia. Happy now?"

Sammy saw Dre nodding and used the short silence to ask Barion about the stag skull. "Are those real gems?" He gestured toward the thing on the wall. Barion grinned.

"Oh yes. I did that myself. I saw this piece by Damian Hirst, the human skull with the diamonds? Are you familiar with it?"

When Sammy nodded, Barion went on. "When I moved here, I found this bag of emerald and ruby splinters and I thought it would fit perfectly to put them on the stag then hang him in the dining room. Very bohemian."

"It is." Sammy nodded. It wasn't something he would want to have in his own home, or Dre's quaint little cottage, come to think of it, but it fit perfectly in this place. "I like the chairs."

Barion puffed his chest. "Also my idea. They used to be a boring red, you know — that brocade red that screams set of *The Tudors* without Jonathan Rhys Meyers as a counterweight to the feeling of moth balls. Don't get me wrong, I like preserving the old, and I did a really good job with this building, even if I do say so myself, but when the old gets too boring or suffocating, it has to be dragged into the twenty-first century — kicking and screaming if necessary."

"Did you just quote Lord Vetinari from *Discworld*, albeit in a roundabout fashion?" When Sammy saw the confused look on Barion's face, he had his answer.

"I told you that Barion isn't much of a reader. His forte is gaming — and TV series. He's kind of an addict." Dre winked at his brother.

"Hence *The Tudors* reference." Sammy grinned. "I have to admit that I'm not an expert in TV series, but I think I know my way around."

Barion pulled out one of the lime-green chairs. Sammy sat down and admired the perfectly set table with two different glasses, rows of gleaming cutlery and plates of the finest, pure-white china. "What's your favorite series then?"

Sammy thought about it while Dre sat down next to him and Barion vanished through yet another door into what had to be the kitchen. When Barion came back with a bowl of steaming *Spaghetti Vongole* and a small pot with what seemed to be the same green spread they had had on their first date in Rome, Sammy smiled happily while Dre handed him a piece of fresh *ciabatta*.

"So, your favorite series?" Barion poured them water and red wine before he sat down. Sammy started putting some of the spread on his *ciabatta*.

"There are a few, actually. My favorite feel-good series is *Gilmore Girls*."

Barion laughed. "I'm with you on that one. You gotta love women who watch an automatic vacuum at the same time in two different places. Something we should try sometime, big bro."

Dre made a face. "Is there a deeper meaning to it or is it just the sheer craziness of the idea itself?"

"Hey, I like that idea." Sammy glared at Dre. "Don't go dissing Lorelai and Rory. They rock!"

"Yeah, Sammy, show Dre who's boss." Barion grinned broadly while he took the spaghetti tongs and started serving them. "What other series do you like?"

"*The Big Bang Theory*. Sheldon is a riot. *Buffy, The Vampire Slayer*, but without the season with Glory. That just wasn't my cup of tea."

Barion shook his head. "I loved *Buffy* through seasons one to four. The rest I only watched because of Spike."

"Oh yes, Spike. I remember your strange obsession with him." Dre chuckled. Barion shot him a nasty look.

"Spike was great. That British accent paired with that platinum-blond hair and those cheekbones sharp enough to cut glass? I would have loved to get acquainted with him."

"You mean you would have loved fucking him through the mattress, little brother."

"Details, details." Barion twirled some spaghetti with his fork. "What else, Sammy? So far, I want to praise you for your good taste."

Sammy grinned. "Let's hope it stays that way. *American Gods*. I loved the book and I can't decide who's sexier, Ian McShane or Ricky Whittle."

"Is there something you want to tell me, *mo grah thu*?" Dre stole a mussel from Sammy's plate. Sammy grinned and gave him a quick kiss on the cheek.

"Do not worry, my demon in shining red. None of them can hold a candle to you."

"That's all I wanted to hear, *mo grah thu*."

"Bah, could you please stop with the sweetness? I'm trying to keep my meal down." Barion's voice was teasing, but when Sammy looked in his direction, he saw the pure longing in the demon's eyes. His heart hurt for Barion, so he tried to distract him.

"I've told you my favorite series. What are yours?"

Barion shoved a fork of spaghetti into his mouth and chewed thoughtfully. "I'm a bit of a swing watcher and a sucker for everything fantasy or historical. So *Game of Thrones* and *The Shannara Chronicles* are high on my list, as well as *Dr. Who*. I can't wait to see what Jodie Whittaker is going to do with the role."

"Yes, her taking over the role was quite the surprise." Sammy nodded and saw Dre rolling his eyes. *Dr. Who* was so far one of the few things where they didn't see eye-to-eye. Dre found the series terrible, while Sammy liked it well enough. And what would a relationship be without some friction here and there?

They finished the delicious meal with easy chatter about TV series, games and actors, and Sammy was getting completely relaxed around Barion. Meeting the family wasn't as bad as he'd thought.

"Before we have our dessert, how about I give you a tour of the house? I'm very proud of it." Barion sounded so eager, and Sammy couldn't wait. All he had seen so far were the huge dining room and the hall leading to it.

Since it was closest, they first went into the kitchen, which was an impressive mixture of old and new. Barion had kept the old fireplace, the massive pipes and broad chimney, as well as the brick construction, and had it all equipped with modern appliances. It was beautiful in a very big way, which made Sammy grateful for Dre's more modest taste. He couldn't imagine cooking in a kitchen like that. They toured the entire house, with the library coming last, at Dre's insistence. When they entered the huge two-story room, Sammy knew why. There was no way he would be leaving here anytime soon.

"Oh my God! It's beautiful. Can I look around?"

Barion nodded with an amused twinkle in his eyes. "Of course. Feel free to explore. To give you some time, how about Dre and I go and get dessert while you have fun in here?"

Sammy looked at him wide-eyed. "You would leave me here alone?"

"Only if you want, *mo grah thu*. And definitely not for long. If you don't feel safe, I can stay with you."

"It's not about me being safe. It's just a lot of trust Barion puts into a complete stranger."

"Hey, man, you're my brother's boyfriend. It's fine. We won't be gone long enough for you to steal anything." Barion winked. "What do you like for dessert?"

The almost two weeks Sammy had spent with Dre had taught him to answer this question truthfully, because there was nothing Dre—and probably Barion—couldn't get him. "I'd like that mousse au chocolat from the little café in Nimes where we went last Sunday. And the *tartuffone* from that *Gelateria* in Rome. You know, the one with the forty different flavors?"

Dre kissed him. "Done, *mo grah thu*. Have fun." He turned to Barion. "You know the *Gelateria*, don't you?"

Barion snorted. "I know all your hunting grounds, big bro. I'll get the *tartuffone*. You go to Nimes. Let's see who's back first." He sliced space and time and was gone in an instant.

"Cheater!" Dre roared and followed his brother. Sammy chuckled and shook his head. He had always wished for siblings, fantasizing about how wonderful his relationship with them would be. Seeing Barion and Dre interact was like all those fantasies had come true.

Sammy turned toward the rows and rows of books. This was heaven. He started wandering between the shelves, pulling out books at random, admiring their leather bindings and reveling in the familiar smell only matured books emanated. If there was an order to them, Sammy couldn't find it. They were roughly in alphabetical order, sometimes apparently using the first letter of the title, then the author's surname, only to switch to the first name. Occult books were mixed with romance novels, essays with guidebooks about gardening, astrology with cookbooks. Sammy itched to catalog them all and order them in a sensible way, but he withstood temptation. This was Barion's library and he was only a guest. Before he could get too worked up, Barion returned, shortly followed by Dre. The bickering of the brothers lured Sammy from behind the shelves.

"You're just a sore loser!" Dre was glaring at Barion, his fangs elongating. He had definitely grown as well. The shirt he was wearing was already ripping at the seams. Barion was not better, his claws digging into the package that Sammy hoped wasn't holding his *tartuffone* — or mashed ice cream if the two demons didn't stop.

"How can I be a loser when I won this round?" Barion was pointing one razor-sharp claw in Dre's direction.

"You're a sore loser because you can't stand to lose and therefore resort to cheating to get your way, just like a toddler."

Barion sneered. "Toddlers aren't as good as me!"

"So you admit it! Ha!"

Sammy decided it was time to save his dessert. "Guys, stop! It doesn't matter who won when you smash the goods. Now calm down, both of you, and let's go back to the dining room and have our sweets. Please?"

Two pairs of glowing red eyes swung in his direction. If anybody had told Sammy only two weeks before that he would stand in the house of a demon, chiding two of them in order to save his food, he would have laughed his head off. But here he was, giving them his best stern look—which, he feared, wasn't much—in hopes of calming the beasts.

Dre was the first to relent. "I'm sorry, *mo grah thu*. I didn't mean to ruin your dessert. I was provoked." He shot a nasty glare in Barion's direction.

"It's not my fault you're getting slow in your old age." Barion huffed but retracted his claws. "Come on. Let's have dessert."

They went back to the dining room, the tension slowly leaving the air between the brothers. By the time they all had their sweet treats in front of them, Barion and Dre were joking again. They enjoyed their food in relative silence, only broken by appreciative moans now and then until they were almost done. When there were only a few spoons of ice cream left on Barion's plate, he looked at them with a determined gleam in his eyes.

"Let's talk about the huge elephant in the room."

Dre narrowed his eyes. "What elephant?"

Barion huffed. "Please, brother. Any idiot can see how close you and Sammy are. What I want to know is why haven't you claimed him yet?" The challenge in Barion's voice was clear, and if Sammy hadn't seen the longing in his eyes before, he would have felt threatened. As it was, he understood why Barion was asking so blatantly. Sammy looked at Dre, saw the question in his eyes and nodded. It was okay with him for Dre to talk about it.

"I haven't claimed Sammy yet because we gave ourselves a two-week period to live our dream. At the end of those two weeks, I'm going to give him my bite and hope he's my mate. But we both agreed we wanted something beautiful to hang on to, should it not be the case."

Barion made a face. "BS. First of all, if this isn't a hidden mate-bond humming between you two, I'll eat my tail. Second —"

"You don't have a tail," Dre interrupted matter-of-factly. Barion rolled his eyes at him. He sounded annoyed. "*If* I had a tail, I'd offer to eat it, but I wouldn't have to, because you two are definitely mates. And second" — he held up his index finger, claw out to prevent Dre from interrupting again — "even if you aren't, it doesn't change the fact of how you feel about each other. Granted, you won't have an eternity together, but still…" He looked at them so full of longing that Sammy immediately felt bad. "You're good for each other. Any idiot can see that. Why not enjoy it while it lasts? You said yourself, Dre, that you've never felt like this. And you seem to be happy, too, Sammy. Embrace it. It's more than many of us have."

"That might be the case, but it's still our decision, brother, and I'd appreciate it if you stayed out of it. By the way, this is the reason why I hesitated to bring Sammy here." Dre sounded more exasperated than annoyed, which was probably a good thing. Barion shook his head, his eyes gleaming redder than the rubies on the stag. "Nothing's ever sure. You know that as well as I do, Dre. The way I see it, you're cowards, both of you. Stop deceiving yourselves and at least own it!"

Dre's fangs started sliding down again, which caused Sammy to interfere. "You're right, Barion. We *are* afraid. I've never loved anybody as much as I love Dre. The mere idea of him not being my forever chills me to the bone. I'm constantly torn between finally finding out and never wanting to know. Don't you get it? Even if we make it work should I not be his mate, it would never be what it is at the moment, that blissful ignorance, the pure love untainted by the realities of the world. That's what we're clinging to. And since we're both mature adults, we decided to put a limit on it."

Dre slung his arm around Sammy's shoulders, pulling him close. Only then did Sammy realize that he was shaking. It felt good to be comforted, to be held like he was the only thing in Dre's world that mattered. Dre surely was the only thing that mattered to Sammy, especially in this moment.

"I'm sorry, Sammy. I didn't mean to upset you." Barion sounded a bit contrite. "It's just that seeing you two together gives me so much hope for finding my own mate. I understand why you're hesitant to find out, but from my point of view, you're wasting the gift Fate has given you. Don't be afraid. You were made for each other. Even if you should not be Dre's mate, which I highly doubt, you will find a way and it will be perfect for you two. Staying in this limbo won't get you anywhere."

Sammy sighed and snuggled closer to Dre. "It's okay, Barion. We know that as well." He twisted his head to look at Dre. "Perhaps we should go home and talk about it?"

Dre nodded. "Seems like a good idea. Thank you, Barion, for the invitation. I'll give you a call as soon as we know."

"You're not angry?" Barion sounded meek.

"No, brother, we're not angry. I, for my part, am just not sure what to think." Dre smiled a bit sadly.

Sammy touched Barion's hand briefly. "It's the same for me. We'll talk soon, okay? Especially about the abysmal order you have to your library." He winked.

Barion huffed in relief, and with a last wave goodbye, Dre brought Sammy back to his kitchen.

Chapter Twelve

"Wow. That was intense." Sammy turned in Dre's arms to snuggle his face against Dre's pecs, something they both enjoyed immensely.

"Yeah, it was. I'm sorry. Barion can be a handful, and he has zero respect for other people's personal space."

"Really?" Sammy winked. "I got the impression that he's the picture of restrained and collected...not meddling at all."

"Which is why I waited so long to introduce you. If I had done this sooner, you'd have run screaming." Dre kissed him lovingly.

"I like to think I would have never run from you, Dre. There's something about you that draws me in. Perhaps I would have made you work for it a bit more, though." Sammy played with Dre's fingers while saying this, clearly teasing him.

Sensing Sammy's inner turmoil, Dre decided it was time to stop with the pussyfooting. "Do you really want to talk about what just happened at Barion's or are we sticking to the initial plan?"

Sammy sighed deeply. "I want to stick to the initial plan. I really do, but it just doesn't make sense, does it? Barion's right. We're just procrastinating." He leaned back in Dre's embrace, meeting his gaze full on. "Let's grab the devil by the horns and do this?"

"You do know there's more than one devil and that they don't necessarily have horns?" Dre lifted one eyebrow. Sammy swatted at his arm.

"Don't try to distract me — and I didn't know. But let's stay focused here." He shuddered. "What's going to happen now? How exactly does this work?"

Dre caressed Sammy's cheek with his knuckles. They had discussed this before, but if his hopefully soon-to-be mate needed to go over it again, Dre wouldn't deny him. Especially since it helped calm his own nerves as well.

"We're going to have penetrative sex for the first time. Ideally, I'm going to take you from behind because of the whole knotting thing — and the bite, of course." Dre gave Sammy what he hoped was a reassuring smile. "When we both reach orgasm and my knot starts to swell, I'm going to bite you here." Dre ghosted his fingers over the crook of Sammy's neck, leaving goosebumps in their wake. "While I ingest your blood, my venom is pumped into your system. If you aren't my mate, you will experience a light drowsiness and the bite will heal just like every other flesh wound you ever got."

Sammy caught Dre's fingers in both his hands and looked at him with a suspicious glint in his eyes. "And if I am? Somehow I'm getting the feeling you're trying to tell me something by not telling me."

Dre sighed. They really were in tune with each other. *Damn!* "If you are my mate—which I'm pretty sure of, by the way—the poison will react with your blood and start reshaping your body so you can become my mate. That process is…uncomfortable."

Sammy raised a brow. "Uncomfortable? Did I miss something?"

Dre winced. "Uhm, I may not have mentioned it before. Very…and painful. I'm sorry."

"You're doing a great job selling this to me," Sammy grumbled. "I mean, seriously, I don't get it. If I'm not your mate, there aren't any problems, but if I am, I get tortured? Were all the paranormal romance books I've read wrong? I want my money back!"

Dre did his best not to smile at those last words. He had a feeling smiles were counterproductive at the moment. He took the route of downplaying mixed with a reasonable explanation. Sammy's brain was scientifically wired, after all.

"The pain doesn't last long, only a few minutes. Afterward it's bliss. I promise. And the books aren't wrong per se, just inaccurate and selective in the information they provide. It's a bit like with pregnancies. If there wasn't all that talk about how wonderful it is to hold a baby in your arm, no woman would ever get pregnant. And if it weren't truly wonderful, no woman would get pregnant twice or more often. Just treat this as a form of slightly misconstrued advertising. The rewards are even greater than described, but getting there takes a few sacrifices."

Sammy stared at him for so long that Dre was half-afraid he would tell him to forget about it all. Then all of a sudden, he started to laugh.

"You're the worst salesman ever, Dre. Has anybody told you that?"

"Not yet."

"Rest assured." Sammy chuckled some more before he turned serious again. "Okay, let's do this. I'm warning you, though, that if this isn't as great as you claim it to be, your ass is toast."

Dre felt a relieved smile tugging at his lips.

"Whatever you say, *mo grah thu*."

Sammy took Dre's hand and led him to his bedroom. They had spent time in there so often during the past week that it no longer felt strange to Sammy. Instead, his heart rate started speeding up and his cock took an interest. It had already learned to expect pleasure from the combination of Dre and the bedroom.

"Do you think we need *The Guide to Successful and Satisfying Sex with a Paranormal*?" Sammy was so nervous that the idea to have something in written form to cling to was more than a bit appealing. Dre kissed him on the top of his head.

"We can read the chapter about demons again, if you want to, though I dare say we already know it by heart. Wouldn't you agree?"

Sammy sighed, grabbed Dre's hands in his own. "You're right. I'm just so nervous, Dre. This is it."

"Yes, this is it. And you know what, *mo grah thu*? I'm no longer afraid. Because this" — he made a gesture that included the entire bedroom — "is us. Barion was right. No matter what happens after my bite, you and I are about to share the most intimate thing between two beings, and there's nobody I'd rather be with at this moment, not even my true mate should you not be it. And that says it all."

Sammy looked into Dre's glowing red eyes, saw the honesty and love in them and felt something inside him unravel, like the world's biggest ball of yarn that had finally decided to set his heart free from its wooly clutches. His heart was beating only for Dre, not only at this moment but since they had first met. He smiled. "You're right. There's nothing to fear. Just us. And I've been dying to have you inside me." He blushed at his own boldness. Dre's deep chuckle didn't help at all.

"Come here, *mo grah thu*. Let me take your clothes off."

Obediently, Sammy kept still while Dre started undressing him. He took his time, got rid of one item of clothing after the other, as if sensing the wild waters of passion that lay before them and wanting to enjoy the calmness of the river they were currently traveling. Sammy was content letting Dre set the pace, relying on his lover's experience. The idea of Dre with other partners still wasn't a welcome one, but if they had both been virgins, this would have been either awkward as hell—no pun intended—or very short or both. As it was, he followed Dre's lead, stepped out of his trousers and underwear when Dre tugged them down his legs and made no attempt to hide his body once he was completely naked. In the beginning, Sammy had been incredibly shy around Dre, whose gorgeous body was every gay man's dream come true. With patience and a good dose of humor, Dre had coaxed him out of his shell and now Sammy was content admiring Dre while he stripped off his own clothes.

When they were both naked, his demon lover gently guided him toward the bed. Once Sammy was on his back under the canopy of pin lights, Dre turned toward the nightstand, rummaging around until he found what he had been looking for. With a triumphant growl, Dre held up the huge bottle of lube they had bought in a sex shop in Amsterdam, as well as the deep red silicone butt plug that had been waiting for them in a specialized shop in Vienna. Sammy felt his cheeks becoming as red as the plug when he thought back to that trip. All he had wanted was a taste of the original *Sacher* cake, but a short stroll through the inner city had led them to this tiny hole-in-the-wall with only one small window in which a gorgeous leather jacket with silver studs had been displayed.

A kiss on his navel brought him back to the here and now. Dre's hot breath was ghosting over his tummy, doing strange things to Sammy's ability to form coherent thoughts. He let his fingers glide over the silver tattoos on Dre's chest and arms, enjoying the slight shiver he got as a reaction.

"Sammy...so good." Dre was pressing his entire body against him, his enormous erection hot on Sammy's already-oversensitive skin. The hard length also reminded Sammy why the plug was necessary. As *The Guide to Successful and Satisfying Sex with a Paranormal* stated —

Being with a demon is always an intense experience, not comparable with any other creature, paranormal or other. A demon's penis is an impressive tool only the bravest and most masochistic take on without preparation. For those of our readers who wish to enjoy the encounter, let us stress how important preparation is. Make sure to have enough lube ready. You're going to need it. We also recommend the use of little helpers, such as plugs, beads or smaller dildos to prepare for the main thing.

When they had first read this paragraph together, Sammy had died of embarrassment, only to be reminded in the following make-out session how very true the words were. Even half hard, Dre's cock was a monster that would be the envy of every locker room, should Dre ever decide to go into sports. Fully erect, it made Sammy's mouth water and his pulse quicken in fear at the same time. Dre slid their bodies together for a few more moments before he sat up and maneuvered Sammy's legs out from under his own to spread them over his massive thighs. Sammy was now completely exposed to Dre's gaze, the cool air in his bedroom an interesting contrast to the hot skin of his demon lover.

Dre was massaging his thighs, slowly coming closer to Sammy's groin and waiting cock. Sammy was already rock-hard, leaking a small puddle of pre-cum on his belly. He had no idea how he was supposed to hold back until Dre entered him—and if he even wanted that.

"Dre," he whimpered.

"Shh-h, *mo grah thu*, it's fine. We have the entire night. All the time in the world." Dre winked while he let the claw of his index finger slide out and scrape over Sammy's cock, just hard enough to elicit a light sting. Sammy moaned, and his hips bucked up without him having any control over it.

"So good for me, Sammy. So good." Dre's voice was a fevered whisper. He closed one hand around Sammy's length, pumping it slowly, while his other hand played with Sammy's balls, teased the flesh between his sack and his hole with his claws.

Sammy started seeing stars and reached for Dre's wrist. "Dre!"

Suddenly, Dre let go of Sammy's cock. He leaned forward to give Sammy a deep, hot kiss, which was a bit wobbly, because he was reaching for something next to Sammy at the same time. When he heard the clicking of a plastic cap being opened, Sammy tensed a bit. Things were getting real. Dre placed a row of sucking kisses on Sammy's neck, chest and belly before he licked over his cock. Sammy arched his back, the elevation of his legs on Dre's thighs providing additional leverage.

Dre groaned and sucked at the tip of Sammy's cock, which was all it took. Sammy came with a desperate wail, his cum shooting into the cavern of Dre's mouth. He was vaguely aware that Dre started to cough but was too caught up in his passion to care. When he slowly came down, Sammy realized that Dre was gasping for air and had tears in his eyes. A clear liquid was dripping down his fingers, and when a huge, cold dollop landed on Sammy's stomach, mixing with his seed, he realized it was lube, which also explained the sheen around Dre's mouth and on his cheeks. He must have gotten the lube on his face when he had his coughing fit. Sammy was still a little dizzy from his orgasm, but his brain finally latched onto what had happened and he couldn't suppress a giggle.

"I'm sorry, Dre. I was just so overwhelmed! I... I didn't mean to... You have lube all over your face... And a bit of sperm. I'm... I'm sorry, but I'm not sorry!" Sammy held his belly because he was laughing so hard. Too late he realized that his arms were now smeared with a mixture of lube and cum, both of which seemed to be getting colder by the second.

Dre shot him a nasty glare before his lips started to twitch as well. "That's what I get for trying to be a compassionate lover. I should have just shoved the plug in, no questions asked. *The Guide* says nothing about lovers coming way too soon."

"We should write a letter to the editors." Sammy tried to keep a straight face, which wasn't easy under the circumstances. "Explain to them how faulty their book is and demand our money back."

Dre giggled. "I have a better idea. Let's write our own book. *The Guide to Successfully Mating a Demon*. I'm sure it'll be a bestseller."

"We sure have plenty of stories to contribute." Sammy grinned. "I'm sorry. I'm just so nervous and excited, and when you put your mouth on me, I just lost it."

Dre leaned down to kiss Sammy with his lube-and-cum-stained lips. The taste was a bit strange, though Sammy didn't complain.

"It's fine, *mo grah thu*. I'm actually flattered how much of an impact I have on you. Now, where were we?" He looked around on the bed, obviously searching for the lube and the plug.

"You wanted to give me this plug to prepare me for you monster cock." Sammy watched as Dre's cock started to twitch. His words must have hit a nerve.

"Sammy, don't say things like that. I'm close, too."

"So it's okay for me to come, but not for you?" Sammy winked.

Dre drew up to his full height, trying for a stern look and failing miserably. "I'm the demon here, *mo grah thu*. I'm supposed to be in control and above my primal needs. One of us has to keep a clear head…" He trailed off, shaking his head. "No, I can't say that with a straight face. Don't laugh!" He looked as if Sammy's giggles were wounding him deeply.

"I'm s-sorry. Let's keep going."

Dre murmured something under his breath and Sammy swore to himself to learn the demon tongue as fast as possible. Before he could dwell on that plan too long, though, the sensation of one of Dre's fingers, coated in cold, cold lube and circling his hole, had him hissing and arching his back again. Dre massaged the wrinkled skin around Sammy's entrance until the lube was fairly warmed up before he pushed one finger in.

Sammy tensed up at the intrusion, even though his cock was obviously very on board with the idea, if the speed with which it grew from semi-hard to fully erect again was anything to go by. Dre placed his other hand on Sammy's belly, massaging him lightly to soothe him. Sammy relaxed, welcoming the thick digit into his body. It was a strange feeling, having something of Dre in such an intimate spot. He wasn't afraid, though, just very turned on. Moaning, he squirmed on the finger and tried to get it deeper.

Dre chuckled, wiggled his finger and played around until Sammy was begging him for a second. They repeated this game with a third finger and Sammy almost came again when Dre finally found his prostate.

"I guess it's time for the plug." Dre had a mischievous glint in his eyes. Sammy stuck his tongue out.

"Let's see how you react when I tap your virgin ass."

Dre pressed a hand over his heart, looking deeply offended. "My ass is off limits. I'm a strong, proud demon warrior who does the pounding!"

Sammy giggled. If they hadn't talked about the possibility of him topping Dre before, he would have almost believed the act. While Dre was not overly enthusiastic to give up his ass, he was willing to do it for Sammy, and Sammy had every intention of trying it at least once, since he was curious how it would feel. If it was only half as good as what he was experiencing now, Dre would be in trouble. Perhaps. If he were honest, Sammy very much liked their roles in sex…so far. He couldn't follow this train of thought any longer. A blunt pressure so different from Dre's fingers alerted him to the appearance of the plug. It was well-lubed and slid in easily, stretching Sammy even wider than Dre's finger had done. It also felt alien, not at all like the rough warmth of Dre. Sammy wasn't sure if he liked it, though he knew it was necessary.

Dre kissed him, and his lips tasted like him again, no longer of lube or cum. "I'm not sure how long we should keep the plug in. I want you prepared to take my cock but not totally exhausted from yet another orgasm, so I can't play with it too much."

"Are you telling me you don't want me to enjoy myself?" Sammy winked to make it clear he was joking. This whole 'getting him ready for Dre' business was a lot more fun than he had imagined.

Dre grinned and held up his right index finger, while his left hand played with the plug, twisting and bumping it, which made it almost impossible for Sammy to follow what Dre was saying. "Mating with a demon is stressful, young man. I want you to be up to the task, which you won't be when you're limp like a noodle."

They both looked down at Sammy's cock, which beat a wild rhythm on his belly with its eager twitching. "I don't think that's an issue." Sammy tried hard for a serious tone and almost managed.

"Not at the moment." Dre growled, twisting the plug again.

Sammy howled when the tip of the plug nudged his sweet spot. His inner muscles clamped down on the toy, desperate for something Sammy was pretty sure only Dre could give him.

"I-I think it's fine. You can take the plug out. I want you now."

Sammy watched Dre's expression shifting between playful, worried and plain hungry. "Are you sure?"

Breathless, Sammy nodded. "Yes, Dre. I'm sure."

Chapter Thirteen

Dre had to close his eyes for a moment to regain control. Playing with Sammy had turned him on to the point where he'd almost come, and only Sammy's untimely orgasm had helped Dre get his urges under control. Seeing his precious lover so vulnerable, so ready for him, stirred feelings in Dre that he'd never thought possible. He wanted to own Sammy, to protect him from all the bad the world had to offer. Sammy belonged in his arms, where he was warm and pampered and safe.

Dre leaned forward to kiss those precious lips while he slowly pulled the plug out, twisting it in the process to stretch Sammy a little more, because no matter how eager his sweet lover sounded, Dre knew his cock would present a serious challenge. Sammy rewarded his troubles with a delicious whimper that Dre inhaled happily.

"As much as I enjoy this, *mo grah thu*, we have to switch positions." Dre murmured the words in Sammy's ear, following them with a lick across the shell. The touch of Sammy's hands on his sides and back was like the sweetest caress and left trails of fire on his skin and sent his thoughts tumbling in his head. He grabbed Sammy's hips, lifted him up until their upper bodies were flush against each other while Sammy's legs dangled freely on either side of Dre. After another passionate kiss, he spun Sammy around, pressed his virgin lover's ass against his belly and slowly lowered Sammy's upper body on the mattress. The sweet, round ass rubbed over his groin and the shapely thighs parted to make room for Dre's massive body. He held Sammy's waist with one hand while he grabbed the lube with the other. While he squirted a generous amount on Sammy's red, twitching hole, Dre wondered for a moment if there was something as too much lube, but one look at his huge erection told him it was needed. He took a moment to play with Sammy's hole, eliciting more of those wonderful moans while opening it even more before he slicked his cock up as well and placed it at Sammy's entrance.

"Easy now, Sammy. Don't forget. We have time." Dre said those words as much for Sammy as for himself. Looking at the tiny hole of his lover and his own huge shaft made him doubt it would ever fit. Slowly, carefully, always on the lookout for the slightest sign of discomfort, Dre pushed into Sammy.

At first, the hole wouldn't let him in. Sammy tensed under his touch, whimpering softly. Dre bent down to press small kisses on Sammy's back, to soothe his lover. "It's fine, *mo grah thu*. Just breathe in deep. When you breathe out, push out as well. That should do the trick."

Sammy moaned and started breathing in so deeply that his chest expanded visibly. Dre's lips twitched in a smile. Sammy did have a tendency to be over-the-top.

He silently begged his lover's forgiveness when the tip of his cock suddenly slipped in. Being over-the-top was definitely helping in this case. Dre bit back a groan when Sammy took him in another half inch. It took all of his self-control to simply provide steady pressure while Sammy worked himself onto his shaft. When he was about halfway into Sammy's tight, wonderful heat, Dre started moving his hips with miniscule motions, testing if Sammy was ready for him to be more active. The desperate moan he got made him bolder, and soon he was gliding back and forth inside Sammy, venturing deeper with each thrust. Sammy wasn't very coherent, but Dre had no trouble understanding him.

"Yes…ah, more… Dre…so good…uhn…this…"

"Sammy…tight…hot…" Dre wasn't that articulate either. He also knew neither of them would last much longer, not when Sammy's inner muscles were gripping him so tight, practically sucking him in now that his body had gotten used to Dre's shaft. He reached for Sammy's right shoulder, pulled him up until his body arched, the touching points Sammy's ass and Dre's groin as well as the crook of Sammy's neck and Dre's lips. He licked over the hot, sweaty flesh, inhaling the sweet scent of Sammy's arousal. They were both panting, ready to cross a line they had been avoiding for a week now.

Dre's fangs elongated and his knot began to swell. "Sammy…close."

"Yes, Dre." Sammy arched his body even more, impaled himself deeper on Dre's cock and pressed against Dre's fangs. "Bite me."

The words triggered Dre's orgasm. His balls drew up, the first spurts of hot semen shot deep into Sammy's body and he sank his fangs into the skin of

Sammy's neck and broke through until he found blood. Sammy screamed in ecstasy, his inner muscles clamping down on Dre as his own orgasm overtook him.

With the first taste of Sammy's blood, combined with his orgasm, Dre knew. His demon came to the fore, eagerly lapping up the essence of their mate while he could feel the venom dripping from his fangs, pulsing into Sammy's veins with each spurt of his cock. Only knowing that he would hurt Sammy kept Dre from letting his fire out. Sammy's body wasn't transformed yet. Dre could fill him with his fire the next time they made love, which he was already looking forward to. Through the haze of his own orgasm and the bliss of knowing that Sammy truly was his, Dre heard the scream of his lover change from ecstatic to one full of pain. The transformation had begun. His venom was burning through Sammy's system, changing his body so they could spend eternity together.

With his swollen knot lodged deeply in his lover's body, Dre held Sammy, whispering soothing words into his ear while Sammy bore the pain of becoming his mate.

Chapter Fourteen

Sammy was in agony, which was good because it meant he was Dre's mate. But it was also — well, agony. Sammy wondered why he had agreed to this. Ah, yes, because he loved Dre, the sex was great and he really wanted to be his mate. *Slightly misconstrued advertising,* ha. This was terrible. Sammy was dimly aware that Dre was holding him tight, whispering soothing nothings in his ear, but he was too consumed by the feeling of burning oil streaming through his veins to be grateful for the support. With every heartbeat, the pain spread and grew, until it was too much to bear and Sammy slipped into near-darkness.

After what felt like an eternity — Sammy couldn't be sure in his agonized state — the pain started to dull and became a deep throbbing at the back of his mind. A soft glow rose around him, enveloped his body with a warmth that was so much better than the fire that had been raging through his system.

Sammy blinked when he thought he saw two figures approaching him through the glow. They stepped into his line of vision and Sammy felt tears streaming down his cheeks when he realized it was his parents. Stella and Moses looked as beautiful as Sammy wanted to remember them, not the mangled, disfigured faces he'd had to identify after the accident.

Stella opened her arms and, without a second thought, Sammy flew into her embrace, breathing in the familiar scent of vanilla while he basked in her love. He felt his father's arms coming around him from behind and knew this was all just a dream, but he was too happy to care. They were here, with him. Nothing else counted.

"My sweet boy." Stella leaned back a bit to press a kiss to his forehead. "My sweet, brave boy."

Sammy smiled through his tears and reached for his father's arm with one hand, while he held his mother with the other. Now that he had them back, he would never let go again. "I missed you so much. So much."

"We know, son. And we're sorry. We never meant to leave you so early."

"It was so hard, going on without your love, without you. But I found friends. Wonderful friends."

His mother kissed him again. "We know, baby. We've watched you all this time. We're so proud of who you've become. And we're here to say goodbye. You've found your happiness with Dre. Good choice, by the way." She winked. "He's almost as good looking as your father. We understand that this is kind of your wedding night, and we wanted to give you our blessings."

Sammy swallowed when the meaning of her words sank in. "I'm not going to see you again, am I?"

"No, son, you won't." His father stepped around, one arm still on Sammy's shoulder, while the other was now draped over Stella's back. "You're the chosen mate of a demon. Your life will be a wonderful, great adventure, and we want you to enjoy every second of it, just how your mother and I enjoyed

every second of ours. We will always love you, never forget that, but it's time for you to truly move on and embrace everything Dre has to offer."

"I don't want to lose you again." Sammy looked at them pleadingly. Stella reached out to sweep a strand of hair from Sammy's face.

"We don't want to lose you either, sweetie. But we have to move on, just as you do. Life doesn't stop with death, you know, and your father and I? We have places to be." She looked up at her husband, a bittersweet smile on her face. "There's so much to see, and you know we always loved to travel."

A sob escaped Sammy. He understood. He really did. It still hurt worse than the venom Dre had pumped into his system. "At least this time I can say goodbye properly." His voice broke. There were no words to describe how he felt, no words to say farewell to the people he had loved most in the world. Luckily, his bond with his parents was so deep that words were not needed. They embraced, leaning their foreheads together, reveling one last time in the bond they'd had. Then they straightened and Stella and Moses each pressed a kiss on Sammy's cheeks.

"We love you, son."

"I love you, Mom, Dad. I wish you a good journey."

Stella smiled sweetly at him. "Thank you, baby."

Sammy watched as the glow surrounding them started to fade, taking his parents with him. He was still sad, mourning for all the things he could never share with them, but having seen them one last time, happy and whole, gave him a sense of peace that he would have never thought possible. Letting them go was one of the most difficult things he had ever done, though instead of being crushed by it, he felt empowered. They had given him their blessing to be with Dre, and Sammy had every intention of taking this gift and making the best of it—as soon as he had a word with Dre about the unpleasantness of mating bites.

Chapter Fifteen

When Sammy finally opened his eyes, Dre felt as if an entire mountain was lifted from his chest. His sweet mate had been unconscious for almost twenty minutes, which was longer than Dre had expected, and he had started crying at some point. Knowing that he couldn't do anything to help Sammy had driven Dre nuts. Sammy groaned and tried to sit up. The movement tugged on Dre's knot, which was still fully swollen inside Sammy's hole. They both whimpered when flashes of arousal went through them.

"How long was I out?" This time, Sammy only moved his head, careful not to jostle the knot again.

"About twenty minutes. I was getting worried." They were still lying on their sides, with Sammy as the little spoon, so he couldn't see Sammy's face, but the mate bond between them was already strong enough for Dre to feel the sadness in his lover.

"I'm sorry. I didn't know it would be that bad."

Sammy sighed. "It hurt like a bitch, Dre, and we're going to talk about your way of selling me this whole mating thing soon enough." He hesitated for a moment. "I saw my parents."

"Oh." That was all Dre could come up with. He knew Sammy's parents were a difficult topic, one that always made Sammy sad. The cross between a sniffle and a laugh Sammy made didn't help Dre to determine what his mate expected of him.

"They gave us their blessing. Mom thinks you're almost as fine as Dad. I'm pretty sure she didn't take a good look at you, because you're better looking than my father."

Dre was relieved to hear the playfulness in Sammy's tone. There was still a tinge of sadness, one that would most probably never go away, because Sammy had loved—and still loved—his parents dearly, but he seemed to have found some kind of closure, for which Dre was grateful.

"Of course I look better. I'm a demon prince. It comes with the territory."

Sammy giggled then groaned. "This knot of yours... How long till the swelling goes down?"

"I haven't got a clue, *mo grah thu*. Do you want to get rid of me already?" Dre nibbled on Sammy's ear.

"No. I was just thinking... Why waste a perfect opportunity?"

"Why indeed? Are you sure you're up for this?"

"Yes, more than sure." Sammy rotated his hips to emphasize his words. Dre groaned and gripped him harder. This was going to be a long night. He couldn't wait.

* * * *

The next morning they were woken by a steady pounding on the door as well as the ringtone from

Sammy's cell. Whenever voice mail took over, there was a short pause, then the ringing started again. Groaning, Dre reached for the annoying device while he cradled his mate close to his chest. Sammy was slowly waking up, but clearly not able to deal with whatever was going on yet.

"What?" Dre did nothing to keep the irritation from his voice. Whoever it was had disturbed their first morning as a mated pair and could go to hell for all Dre cared.

"Ooh, someone's a grumpy ass this morning. Where's Sammy?" Dre wasn't sure if it was Declan or Troy on the phone and he didn't really care.

"Still asleep. What do you want?"

"Who pissed in your cereal? Never mind, it's already past nine, and the shop's still closed. Troy and I need our coffee fix."

Dre took the cell off his ear for a moment to stare at it with his mouth hanging open before he put it back. "You're waking us up because you need Sammy to make your coffee? Are you nuts?"

"Interesting question. Depending on who you ask, the answer differs. And we need Sammy's coffee. He's the only one who gets it right."

Dre opened his mouth to give a sharp answer when Sammy reached out and took the cell from him. He looked adorable with his sleep-tousled hair and the lips still swollen from kissing. "I'll be down in a minute. Stop making such a ruckus." With that, Sammy ended the call and started getting out of bed. Dre managed to catch his wrist.

"Are you seriously telling me you're going down there to make them coffee?"

Sammy smiled weakly. "It's not that I *want* to go down there. But believe me, it's better in the long run. These two won't stop pestering us until they have their caffeine fix. Do you really want to spend the morning waiting for what they will come up with to get me down there?"

Dre pondered the question for a moment. He didn't like the pictures his mind provided. "Fine. But I'm coming with you." He let go of Sammy's hand and bent down to pick up his trousers. Sammy was already putting his on. Neither of them bothered with a shirt since they had every intention of getting back to bed again once the terrible two were dealt with. Dre followed Sammy into the shop and opened the shop door for Declan and Troy while Sammy went behind the counter to start the coffee machine. The werewolves sauntered in as if it were perfectly normal to harass other people for coffee at the butt-crack of dawn. Well, early in the morning.

"Had a good night?" Declan eyed Dre's naked torso. Troy made a beeline for Sammy. Dre was just formulating his answer when a sudden gasp made him turn toward Troy and Sammy. Troy was staring at Sammy with big eyes, the outstretched index finger of his right hand trembling slightly in the air. Declan ran to his friend — lover? partner in crime? Dre was never sure — to see what had him so excited. Sammy was looking at both of them, clearly wanting to know what the issue was. Then Dre realized it too.

Sammy's torso was covered in silver tattoos, marking him as Dre's mate. The sight made his cock instantly swell and he felt himself growing as his demon form took over. Careful to keep his wings close to his body, Dre stepped to the counter to touch

Sammy's naked chest where the words *Mate of Dresalantion, Prince of the Demon Realm* were engraved in the demon tongue. He couldn't believe he hadn't noticed the tattoos sooner, though he had been otherwise occupied during the night, and when Declan and Troy had woken them, it had taken all his concentration not to strangle the two werewolves.

He couldn't suppress his proud grin. "You look beautiful, *mo grah thu*."

Sammy obviously still hadn't caught on. He looked from Dre to Declan and Troy and back, before his gaze finally went to his naked chest.

"Oh."

"Oh? That's all you have to say?" Troy almost squeaked. "You're mated, Sammy! You found your true mate! That's so cool. Congratulations!"

"Yes, congratulations to both of you." Declan smiled broadly, offered Dre his hand after a moment's hesitation when he realized Dre was in his demon form. Dre grinned and took the offered hand then pulled Declan into a hug.

"Thank you. We're very happy."

Troy was next to embrace him while Declan pulled Sammy from behind the counter and against his chest. "I'm sorry we woke you up. If we had known it was your mating night, we wouldn't have bothered you...probably."

At least Declan was honest. "It was a spontaneous decision. It's fine." Faced with the genuine joy of the werewolves, Dre found it hard to stay mad at them.

"Okay, let me get your coffee ready then you can run off and tell the others while my mate and I go back to bed." Sammy disentangled himself from Troy's embrace and went behind the counter again to make the coffee. Once the werewolves had their caffeine, Sammy closed the door, put a sign in the window explaining the shop would be closed until Tuesday, then they went back upstairs. Since they were already up, they had a quick breakfast before they showered together. After that, Dre spent the rest of the day exploring the tattoos on Sammy's body and getting his mate intimately acquainted with his fire and his knot.

Life was perfect.

Chapter Sixteen

Sammy was standing in front of the mirror in his bedroom, fussing with his jeans and trying not to think about the fact that he would be meeting Dre's father half-naked. Apparently, it was customary for the mates of demons to show off their tattoos so everybody knew who they belonged to. When Dre had hinted that the tattoos on Sammy's legs and private parts were obscured by the jeans, he had only given his mate a withering look and Dre had wisely chosen not to press the subject. They had spent Saturday and the first half of Sunday in wonderful, domestic, sexy bliss until Sammy's friends had showed up to celebrate their mating with an extended brunch. It was Monday evening now and they were expected at Barion's mansion to celebrate again, this time with Dre's family.

"Don't worry, *mo grah thu*. My father is more than happy for us. He can't wait to get to know you." Dre slung his arms around Sammy and pressed a kiss on the top of his head. "He's going to love you."

"I hope so. You really have to start teaching me your language. I don't want your father to think I'm not putting in the effort."

Dre turned him around to look him square in the eyes. "Sammy, my love, I'm thrilled you want to learn the demon tongue, don't get me wrong, but I don't want you to think you're under any obligation to do so. You're as much my mate as I am yours. This goes both ways, lover."

Sammy sighed. "I know. I really do. It's just..." He couldn't bring himself to say it. He didn't have to. Through their mate bond, Dre got it.

"This is the only family you have left, apart from your friends. I understand, *mo grah thu*."

Sammy had to swallow a lump in his throat. Thinking of his parents still made him sad, though it was getting better. "I don't want to replace them, certainly not, but I could— I could use a father who's still there, you know?"

"Nobody thinks you're replacing them, Sammy. And I'm sure my father will be more than happy to be there for you."

"I hope so." Sammy straightened. "I think we better get going before I have a nervous breakdown. I'm sure Barion is already waiting for us."

Dre laughed. "Oh yes, he is. He's been here twice already, asking what's taking us so long."

Sammy shuddered. "I guess I'm glad I took so long in the shower."

"You bet you are. My little brother is like a kid on a sugar high."

With one last glance at the mirror — yes, he was still half-naked — Sammy embraced Dre while his mate — *his mate* — sliced time and space to get them to Barion.

Somehow, Sammy had hoped to have some time to calm his nerves—even though deep down he knew that would have never worked—before meeting Dre's father, but he wasn't that lucky. Alerion was standing right next to Barion in the hall where Sammy and Dre had materialized. Dre tightened his hold on Sammy before he dragged him toward his waiting father and brother. Barion looked as if he were about to vibrate out of his skin, yet held himself back, probably because of the imposing figure next to him. There was no doubt that Alerion was Barion and Dre's father. Their features were so similar. Alerion did look more like a brother, not a father, though it was hard to tell his age—how did demons age, anyway?—because he was completely black with golden tattoos and a shock of white hair. Sammy was acutely aware of his near-nakedness in front of his father-in-law. To make matters worse, he felt a flush creeping up his neck, surely making him look like a tomato.

"Father, this is Sammy, my destined mate. Sammy, this is my father, Alerion, the king of all demons."

Alerion smiled broadly and reached out with his hand. Sammy took it automatically, even though his brain had just fried. "No need to be so formal, son. Hello, Sammy, I would very much prefer it if you called me Alerion or, if you feel comfortable with it, Dad. I can't tell you how happy I am Dre found you."

Sammy tried to shake hands with the demon king, while his mouth went on autopilot. "I don't even know if I'm supposed to bow, Your High…uhm, Dad. Dre, why didn't you tell me how to greet your father properly?"

"Yes, Dre, why didn't you tell him?" Barion needled.

"Watch it, Barion." Dre sounded slightly annoyed.

"Quiet, both of you." Alerion used his hold on Sammy's hand to pull him into a hug. "I already like you, Sammy. You're funny. For the protocol, there's no need for you to bow. Unlike my rowdy sons and subjects, I don't have the feeling I have to assert my dominance over you." He stepped back and winked. Sammy grinned.

"No, Dad, most certainly not. I know how that works. Declan and Troy had a hard time restraining themselves in the beginning."

Alerion raised a brow. "Your former lovers?"

Sammy felt his cheeks redden. "Gods, no! They're members of my book club—and also werewolves. Alphas. Did you know that alpha and omega are originally the first and last letter of the Greek alphabet and were used in Christian mythology to describe Jesus as the beginning and the end of everything? I think it's rather funny that it's also used to describe the strongest and the weakest member in a wolf pack, though if you think about it, it makes sense, in a weird kind of way… I'm blabbering, aren't I? Dre?"

"No, *mo grah thu*, you're just being your adorable self. I would never accuse you of blabbering!" Dre did his best to hide his smile.

"That's because Dre is the king of blabbering himself." Alerion patted his son fondly on the back. "Let's get comfortable in the dining room. I hope you didn't cook yourself, Barion?" He shot his youngest son a hard look.

"I don't know why everybody keeps bringing this up. It was an accident, an honest mistake. Come to think of it, it's your fault for letting me into the kitchen unsupervised at such a young age!"

"Young age? You were over six hundred at the time! Hardly an unsuspecting youth. And you insisted!" Alerion's jaw was set in a way Sammy knew only too well. He felt himself relaxing more and more. He enjoyed a good show, just like everybody else.

"I wanted to make something nice for you, to show my love! Geez, one little mistake..." Barion grumbled.

"It's the thought that counts, little brother. Definitely. And I'm sure Father will never forget your show of filial appreciation."

"No, I won't, Barion. That memory is something unique and you have given it to me." Alerion sounded almost sweet. Only the telltale twinkle in Dre's and his father's eyes told Sammy that they weren't serious. Barion huffed.

"Tell me at least you're on my side, Sammy. I obviously can't count on these two."

Sammy regarded Barion for a long moment. He felt the eyes of Dre and Alerion on him, waiting for his reaction. "I'm sorry, Barion. Until I know the full story, I can't make an informed decision. You'll have to tell me first."

Barion's eyes widened. "Forget it! You're as bad as them. I'm going to look for a new family."

They had reached the dining room with the stag and the green cushions. An assembly of Italian appetizers was spread out on the table and made Sammy's mouth water.

"Can you do that after we have dinner? This looks great!"

"You're a perfect fit for this family." Barion brushed past him to pull out a chair for Sammy, retaining an indignant expression. Sammy grinned and sat down.

"Thank you, Barion. And I didn't mean it, you know? You're great, and if you want, I can ask Mavis and Maribel to give you some cooking lessons."

Barion pretended to think about this offer. "You know, I'll pass on the cooking lessons, but could I perhaps come to your next book club meeting?"

A snort from Dre prevented Sammy from answering. "You barely read. Why would you want to go to a book club meeting?"

Barion flipped off his brother. "I happen to be an awesome reader. I just don't advertise. Plus, seeing you two so happy together had made me realize that I have to get out more. Humans can be tedious, as we all know. Your friends are all paranormals. That should make it easier for me to start with the whole getting-to-know-people thing."

"I understand your reasoning. I really do." Sammy patted Barion's hand. "I'm just not sure if this is a good idea. My friends weren't too happy about me hooking up with Dre." When he saw the devastated look on Barion's face, Sammy relented. "Of course you can come. I'll tell them as soon as we're home. Our next meeting is this Wednesday and we're reading Wolfgang Hohlbein, *The Witcher of Salem*, and the *Cthulhu Cycle* by H. P. Lovecraft."

"I'm going to read them! Or at least the summary on Wikipedia. Thank you, Sammy!" Barion pressed a kiss on Sammy's cheek before quickly dancing out of reach of Dre's claws.

"Hands off my mate!"

They spent the rest of the evening eating and chatting happily. Alerion was even nicer than Dre had told him, and when he started telling childhood stories about his sons, Sammy had to laugh so hard that his ribs began to hurt. They parted with the promise to meet again soon, this time at Alerion's home in Switzerland where he would treat Sammy to a traditional Switzer cheese fondue, complete with white bread and schnapps.

Back in Sammy's apartment, they undressed and slipped under the covers after a quick stop at the bathroom.

"Now, that wasn't so bad, was it?" Dre pulled Sammy's back against his broad chest, massaging his upper thigh with his big hands. Sammy couldn't suppress a groan. Being touched by Dre was as good as touching him, and he was already addicted to both sensations. Having a true mate definitely was bliss.

"No, it was fun. I like your father." Sammy hesitated. "I didn't want to ask while we were at Barion's, since I do remember that this is a sore topic, but is there a reason your oldest brother wasn't there?"

Sammy felt Dre tensing up behind him before he sighed deeply. "You're right. This is a difficult topic for me, and for dad and Barion as well. Quirion has always been — different. He's very bookish, but not in a fun, nerdy way like you and me. More in a 'once he gets caught, he doesn't look up' way. It's very hard to get him out of his home, and while he is happy I found my mate, that's still no reason for him to abandon his studies. Don't take it personally. We have stopped doing that centuries ago. It's just the way he is."

"I'm sorry. It must be hard not being able to connect with your brother."

"It was, in the beginning. I've made my peace with it. The way I see it, Quirion is a constant in my life, something that never changes, that always waits for me in the same place, which is good at least for me. And I think he's happy, so why should I force my ideas of happiness on him, even when his way of living strikes me as odd, to put it mildly?"

"You're a great brother. A great mate. I love you, Dre."

"And I love you, Sammy. Now, are you up for some honeymoon sex? Because I'm ready to go." To emphasize his words, Dre nudged Sammy with his huge cock. A whimper escaped Sammy. Strictly speaking, he was too tired for action. Strictly speaking. On second thought, he was more than willing to roll around with his mate.

Chapter Seventeen

"You think this is a good idea?" Now that the book club meeting was actually happening, Sammy seemed to have second thoughts on Barion joining them.

"No, it's probably not. But we both love Barion, so we can't tell him not to come and the others said it's okay. We just have to take Mavis' and Maribell's baskets from them, in case they come armored again." Dre wasn't sure what to think of Barion's sudden interest in meeting people, but when he came to the book club, at least Dre could keep an eye on him. If Barion got into trouble, Dre would be there to help — or stop — him. Unless he pissed off the witches. Then his little brother would be on his own. Dre loved Barion, but he wasn't suicidal, not when he'd finally found his mate. He took Sammy's hand. "Let's just see what happens. We can't change it now anyway."

"I love your pragmatic view on the world." Sammy started making the drinks for his friends while Dre put some left-over pastries on a plate. Today was Emilia's turn to bring sweets. As Sammy had informed him, the vampire tended toward more exotic food, like Japanese *mochi* ice cream, *wagashi* and *sata andagi*. While Dre liked to try new things, he was a traditionalist when it came to his pastries, meaning he preferred cookies and pie and muffins over anything else. The plate with the pastries was his emergency ration.

A soft rustling at the tables let Dre turned around. Milo had already gone home. The kid had to study for another test, and the shop had been empty. Since he hadn't heard the door chimes, Dre assumed his brother had arrived. "Barion." He stopped short. It wasn't his brother but Jon standing there, his hands folded in front of his body. "Oh, hi, Jon. I'm sorry. I forgot you come from downstairs. I was expecting my brother."

Jon opened his mouth to say something but was cut short by Barion's booming voice. "Did I hear my name?" Barion stepped forward from the section with the manga comics, his eyes gleaming happily.

"Yes. I mistook Jon for you. Jon, this is Barion, my younger brother. Don't take anything he says seriously, and just in case he pisses you off, don't forget that we have different mothers and I'm mated to your landlord. Barion, this is Jon. He's a nice guy, so don't bother him with your usual crap."

"Geez, brother, I feel so loved." Barion turned to Jon, offering him his hand, only to pull it back when he seemed to remember what Dre had told him about the zombie's aversion to touching. "Hi, Jon. I'm so sorry you only had my brother as a role model for demons so far. I can assure you that we weren't all born with a stick up our asses. Some of us are actually fun to be around."

Jon grinned broadly. "Hi, Barion. I like you. You're funny. Who do you think should end up on the Iron Throne?"

Barion's eyes started to gleam. "A man after my heart. Daenerys, of course, with Jon as her loving husband and Drogon and Rhaegal to protect their children. Tell me, what do you think about Lagertha?"

"I love her. A strong woman, who knows what she wants and who has no qualms taking it. Though I do have a weak spot for Aslaug. I think she was misrepresented in the series."

Barion smiled broadly and gestured toward one of the couches. "Shall we sit? I can feel a longer discussion in our immediate future."

Jon nodded shyly before sitting down next to Barion. The two started chatting like they'd known each other forever. Dre turned to Sammy with raised brows. All he got was a shrug.

When Sammy was done making everybody's favorite beverage, the others started trickling in, as if they had smelled it. Mavis and Maribell were the first, followed by Amber and Emilia, who had indeed brought an assortment of Japanese sweets, which made Dre grateful for the pastries he had secured. Last were Troy and Declan, who immediately snatched two of the green *mochi* ice creams, happily munching on them while they settled next to Amber. Once everybody was seated, Sammy cleared his throat. "Welcome, everybody, to our book club meeting. Over there is Barion, Dre's little brother, who has joined us today to see if the book club is for him."

Barion waved, meeting the gaze of everybody. Declan and Troy waved back, Emilia and Amber gave a nod, and Mavis and Maribell just stared. Their purses were too small to host a lot of curses, so Dre allowed himself to relax slightly. Sammy went on, recapitulating what they had done during the last meeting before introducing the new topic. "Now what were your impressions of the *Cthulhu Cycle* by H. P. Lovecraft?" He looked around.

Both of Barion's brows arched up. "I've meant to ask this before, brother. Wasn't Lovecraft that human Aunt Corrallione hooked up with for some time?"

Dre rolled his eyes. Leave it to Barion to ruin his big surprise. "Yes, Barion. She was. And thank you. I've meant to mention this little tidbit casually during discussion. Thanks to you, my grand entrance is ruined."

"Wait, Lovecraft actually knew a demon?" Amber's eyebrows almost reached her hairline and she looked at lot more elegant doing it than Barion.

"'Knew' is one way of putting it," Barion huffed. "They were fucking like bunnies in the spring."

"Barion! Watch your language." Dre threw his brother an angry look.

"Don't mind the language. We've all heard worse." Emilia grinned. "But knowing that Lovecraft actually had a reliable source for his stories sheds a different light on it all. Now, Dre, Barion, help us find out what is true and what is fiction in the *Cthulhu Cycle*."

"This is so cool! I've always wondered how Lovecraft managed such great details." Jon sounded so excited that it had Dre smiling. He truly liked the zombie and seeing him happy woke warm feelings in Dre's chest.

"Well, I guess it's time to share some stories, don't you think, Barion?" He winked at his brother, who returned the gesture.

"Don't you dare fool us, boys!" Mavis gazed at them sternly. "This is too good to be just a tall tale."

"We would never dare, ma'am." Dre bowed, took a sip from his tea and leaned back in his seat, an arm over Sammy's shoulder. "Where do we start?"

"How about Nyarlathotep? I always wondered what Lovecraft had to smoke in order to make him up." Declan stole the last *mochi* ice cream.

"Yes, Nyarl. He actually has a real counterpart in the demon realm, though he's imprisoned for life—which in our case means forever. Bastard deserves no less. As for his role in the *Cthulhu Cycle*..."

The evening just flew by and before Dre knew it, he and Sammy were closing the shop behind their friends while Barion insisted on accompanying Jon down to the cellar. His brother had made it clear that he would go directly home afterward, which left Dre and Sammy in blissful solitude.

"What do you say, mate of mine? Shall we go upstairs and deal with the dishes tomorrow?" Dre kissed Sammy's cheek.

Sammy only hesitated for a second before he abandoned the dishes and went into his arms. "I think Mavis and Maribell have decided I can do the cleaning up now that I have help."

"They helped you before?"

Sammy made a vaguely magical gesture with his hands. "They cheated. It drove Declan and Troy nuts with jealousy."

"I can imagine! But they're right. You have me now, your strong demon warrior, and the mess I can't handle has yet to be made."

"Oh, I'd love to make a mess, my love." Sammy waggled his eyebrows. Dre felt his cock taking an immediate interest.

"I can help you with that, *mo grah thu*." He whisked Sammy in his arms and didn't bother with the stairs. One swipe of his claw and they were in Sammy's — *their* — bedroom, ready to create the mess of messes after a wonderful evening spent with their friends.

Life couldn't get much better.

Want to see more like this?
Here's a taster for you to enjoy!

Wanted: Demon Familiar
Bellora Quinn and Sadie Rose Bermingham

Excerpt

Neil set the bushel of summer squash into the panel van with the rest of the produce ready to go to market tomorrow morning and jumped down. Mr. Yaetz patted him on the back. "That's the last one. Good job, Neil. You best head home now. Don't want to get caught outside the wards after nightfall, 'specially not in that fancy car."

Neil stifled a wince and forced himself not to look around to see who might have overheard the mention of his 'fancy car'. Mr. Yaetz didn't mean anything by it, but the car was a sore point with his co-workers at the small greenhouse and urban farm lot. None of them had their own vehicle, much less a sleek convertible sports car. Explaining that it was his mother's, not his, hadn't stopped the digs about his 'slumming with the common folk' or brought him any closer to the camaraderie the rest of them shared.

"Thanks, Mr. Yaetz. I'll see you tomorrow," Neil told him and turned toward the front lot. He glanced at the horizon automatically, judging how much time he had. About forty-five minutes, maybe an hour. More than enough for the short drive home. He wasn't likely to come across any shadow beasts here on the outskirts of the city but a pack hunting farther afield was always a possibility. Of course, if he did run across shadow beasts, they would have to catch him first and the Maserati was both fast and agile.

Neil slid behind the wheel and the powerful engine purred to life. With the sun slowly sinking behind him, he swung the car out onto the road and headed for home.

As expected, Neil pulled into the driveway with plenty of daylight left and no encounters with any creatures that came out after dark. Climbing the front steps, his thoughts preoccupied with a shower and dinner, he almost missed the broken seal on his front door. He stopped cold. The warding glyph, usually a subtle shimmering gold, was inert, dull gray and cracked with lines of black. A sick knot cramped in his belly and Neil pressed his thumb down on the latch and pushed the door open but hesitated on the threshold.

"Mom?"

He listened. No answer.

Neil stepped into the foyer and slowly moved into the hall. A picture had been knocked off the wall and the broken glass from the frame glittered in the fading sunlight streaming in behind him.

"Mom?" he called again, louder.

Something crashed in the kitchen, the metallic clatter of pans hitting the tile floor. Neil ran in that direction.

His mother screamed, "Neil, get out! Get out!"

Heart hammering, he skidded into the kitchen. A black-clad, hooded man held on to his struggling mother. Another man stood next to them with a curved knife in his hand—his eyes were flat black and icy cold as they slid over him. Neil rushed them, yelling, "Get away from her!" The man with the knife lifted his free arm and flung the outstretched fingers of his empty hand at him. Neil hit the stop spell so hard it jarred him from teeth to toes, knocking him on his ass.

"Neil!" his mother shrieked.

He lifted his head in time to see the man who had floored him lift the knife and draw it down the side of her throat and across her shoulder in two professional, vicious slashes. The other man let her go as her eyes went wide and her hands flew up to clutch at the wounds. The blood didn't spray everywhere like it did in the movies. It welled up in a gush of red that soaked the front of her shirt as she choked and gasped then fell down on her knees.

"Mom! No!" Neil scrambled to his feet. The two men moved toward him in unison as his mother crumpled, face down on the floor. Her body sounded like a wet rag hitting the tiles and a shocking pool of red spread under her.

"Take him," the one holding the bloody knife said. His voice was low, emotionless and without accent, like an automaton in one of the old films they occasionally streamed when the comms satellite was functioning.

On autopilot, Neil grabbed the pendant that hung on the chain around his neck and ripped it off, throwing it on the floor. The man reached to stop him, but it was too late. The glass pendant shattered and a wall of noxious smoke rose between him and the killers. It wouldn't hold them long, a minute if he was lucky. Probably less. He turned and ran back down the hall, fleeing the house.

He stumbled down the steps and fumbled the keys from his pocket, hitting the lock button. He yanked the door open and was shaking so badly he dropped the keys on the floor.

"Fuck! Fuck!" He reached down and his fingers just touched the ring as the killers came running out of the front door. Neil grabbed the keyring and jammed the right key in the ignition. For one horrible second, he was sure it wouldn't start even though he'd just driven the car home. The engine turned over as smooth as a kitten's purr and he slammed the shifter in reverse just as the man with the blade grabbed the driver's door handle. Neil put his foot down on the pedal. The tires squealed and the car shot backward down the driveway and into the street.

Blood pounded in his ears, almost drowning out the engine sounds as he threw the car into drive and floored the gas, clutching the steering wheel hard enough to turn his knuckles white. He looked in the rear-view mirror as he sped away. They would come after him. He turned at the next intersection. Then turned again. And again. He tried to focus on what to do next but all he could see was the shock and anguish on his mother's face before she fell, and that bright pool of red spreading out under her. He looked in the mirror again but saw no sign of the men that had killed her. That didn't mean anything. They could come, he knew it. He was heading out of the city following pure instinct, but now he slowed the car for just a moment. At the next turn, he doubled back the way he'd come.

Out of the city might seem safer, but it wasn't. He had little money and the car would take him only so far. He needed resources.

He forced his fingers to relax on the steering wheel but his hands still shook. When he took a breath, it was shaky too. The red had been so stark against her blonde hair. Her eyes...had they been blank before she fell or after she hit the floor? No. No he couldn't think of that now. He raised and hand and swiped at his wet cheeks.

Bone Men. Their name whispered across Neil's mind in his father's voice, from one of his many lessons. Assassins. Twisted by the sorcery that enhanced them, marked by the lives they took. Had she been their target? Was her death retribution for something his father had done? Or…or were they there for him?

His mind raced as fast as his pulse and the car he was driving. He took another deep breath and eased his foot back off the pedal a few degrees. He needed a clear head. He needed a plan. But first he needed somewhere to hide. Instinct told him to find someone he trusted, but his training overrode that idea. He could hear his father's voice in his ear again. *Trust no one, Nielob. If they come for you, go to ground. Speak to no one you know. Hide and wait. I will find you.*

Not if he could help it. If he had his way, he'd lose both the Bone Men and his father, for good. The car would get him a good distance but he couldn't keep it. It was traceable. He'd drive into the city, find someone he could sell the car to for scrap and use the money to get a ticket to as far away as it would take him.

He couldn't take the car directly to a salvage yard without a title, too risky. He needed a fence. Months ago, while he'd been watering seedlings at work, he'd overheard Carl bragging about how his uncle was going to get a real car, one with a combustion engine. No one had believed him and Carl had gotten mad. Insisted his uncle knew a guy that dealt in contraband autos in the city. Hammersfell Road, next to the old Ackard Motors factory. There was a warehouse where they had raves. The fence organized them. Neil had no way of knowing if the bragging was just lies, but he had filed the information away anyway. His chin gave an odd quiver and the tightness in his throat squeezed hard enough to choke him. No. He couldn't give in to tears now. He couldn't afford to let out the sobs that threatened him. A safe place first. The grief tasted of bitter acid and wanted to strangle him, but he swallowed it down and kept going.

PUBLISHING

Sign up for our newsletter and find out about all our romance book releases, eBook sales and promotions, sneak peeks and FREE romance books!

About the Author

Xenia Melzer was born and raised in a small village in the South of Bavaria. As one of nature's true chocoholics, she's always in search of the perfect chocolate experience. So far, she's had about a dozen truly remarkable ones. Despite having been in close proximity to the mountains all her life, she has never understood why so many people think snow sports are fun. There are neither chocolate nor horses involved and it's cold by definition, so where's the sense? She does not like beer either and has never been to the Oktoberfest— no quality chocolate there.

Even though her mind is preoccupied with various stories most of the time, Xenia has managed to get through school and university with surprisingly good grades. Right after school she met her one true love who showed her that reality is capable of producing some truly amazing love stories itself.

While she was having her two children, she started writing down the most persistent stories in her head as a way of relieving mommy-related stress symptoms. As it turned out, the stress-relief has now become a source of the same, albeit a positive one.

When she's not writing, she translates the stories of other authors into German, enjoys riding and running, spending time with her kids, and dancing with her husband.

Xenia loves to hear from readers. You can find her contact information, website details and author profile page at https://www.pride-publishing.com